SIMON AND SCHUSTER

First published in Great Britain in 2013 by Simon & Schuster UK Ltd
A CBS COMPANY

Copyright © 2013 by Darren Shan

Illustrations © Warren Pleece

1 3 5 7 9 10 8 6 4 2

Simon & Schuster UK Ltd
1st Floor
222 Gray's Inn Road
London
WC1X 8HB

www.simonandschuster.co.uk

Simon & Schuster Australia, Sydney
Simon & Schuster India, New Delhi

A CIP catalogue copy for this book
is available from the British Library.

HB ISBN: 978-0-85707-760-8
EBOOK ISBN: 978-0-85707-763-9

Printed and bound by CPI Group (UK) Ltd, Croydon, CR0 4YY

For:

Mrs Shan!!!

OBE (Order of the Bloody Entrails) to:

Elisa Offord – queen of the mutant babies

Edited in a swanky city apartment by:

Venetia Gosling

Kate Sullivan

Darren Shan is represented by

the urban ladies and gentlemen

of the Christopher Little Agency

THEN . . .

A man with owl-like eyes visited Becky Smith one evening and told her there were dark times ahead. A few days later zombies attacked her school and one of them ripped B's heart from her chest. But because the zombies didn't eat her brain, she came back to life soon after her death, as a monster.

Most zombies were unthinking killing machines, but some regained their senses and became revitaliseds, undead creatures who could reason as they had before they died. But to stay that way, they needed to eat human brains. Otherwise they regressed and became savage reviveds again.

Months after her transformation, B recovered her mind. She was being held prisoner in an underground complex, guarded by a team of scientists and soldiers. She was part of a group of revitalised teenagers. They called themselves zom heads. When B refused to cooperate with her captors, all of the zom heads were denied brains as a punishment.

Shortly before the teenagers lost control of their senses, a nightmarish clown and a pack of mutants invaded the complex. The clown's name was Mr Dowling. B had never seen him before, but she had crossed paths with a few of the mutants.

Mr Dowling's followers uncaged the zombies and slaughtered any humans they could lay their hands on. The zom heads made a break for freedom. When one of them was found to be a living boy who had been disguised as a zombie, the others ripped his brain from its skull and tucked in. Only B resisted.

As B mourned the loss of her friend, a soldier called Josh Massoglia tracked down the zom heads and instructed his team to burn them to the bone. But for some reason he spared B and let her go.

Weary and close to her conscious end, she staggered through a tunnel, out of the darkness of the underground complex, into daylight and a city of the living dead.

NOW . . .

ONE

The sunlight is blinding to my undead, sensitive eyes. I try to shut my eyelids, forgetting for a moment that they stopped working when I was killed. Grimacing, I turn my head aside and cover my eyes with an arm. I stumble away from the open door and the nightmare of the underground complex, no idea where I am or where I'm going, just wanting to escape from the madness, the killing and the flames.

After several steps, my knee strikes something hard and I fall over. Groaning, I push myself up and lower my arm slightly, forcing my eyes to focus. For a while the world is a ball of lightning-sharp whiteness. Then, as my pupils slowly adjust, objects materialise through the haze. I ignore the pain and turn slowly to assess my surroundings.

I'm in a scrapyard. Old cars are piled on top of one another, three high in some places. Ancient washing machines, fridges, TVs and microwave ovens are strewn around. Many of the appliances have been gutted for spare parts.

A few concrete buildings dot the landscape, each the size of a small shed. I came out through one of them. I guess that the others also house secret entrances to the underground complex.

I pick my way through the mess of the scrapyard, steering clear of the concrete sheds, ready to run if any soldiers appear. I still don't know why I was allowed to leave when the others were killed. Maybe Josh felt sorry for me. Or maybe this is part of a game and I'm going to be hauled back in just when I think that freedom is mine for the taking.

A stabbing pain lances my stomach. I wheeze and bend over, waiting for it to pass. The ground swims in front of my eyes. I think that I'm about to lose consciousness and become a full-on zombie, a brain-dead revived. Then my vision clears and the pain passes. But I know it's only a short respite. If I don't eat some brains soon, I'm finished.

I search for an exit but this place is a maze. I can't walk in a straight line because it's full of twisting alleys and dead ends. It feels like I'm circling aimlessly, trapped in a web of broken-down appliances.

I lose patience and climb a tower of cars. On the roof of the uppermost car I steady myself then take a look around, shielding my eyes with a hand. Exposed to the sunlight, my flesh starts itching wherever it isn't covered, my arms, my neck, my face, my scalp, my bare feet. I grit my teeth against the irritation and keep looking.

The scrapyard feels like a cemetery, as if no one has been through it in years. I came out of one of the secondary exits. The main entrance must be housed elsewhere, maybe in a completely different yard or building. I'm glad of that. I don't want to run into Mr Dowling or any of his mutants as they're trotting back to wherever it is they hailed from.

The yard is ringed by a tall wire fence. I spot a gate off to my left, not too far away, maybe fifteen metres as the crow flies. I start to climb down, to try and find a path, then pause. One of the concrete sheds is close by and there are a few piles of cars between that and the fence. If I leap across, I can get to the gate in less than a minute.

I gauge the distance to the shed. It's leapable, but only just. If I don't make it, the ground is littered with all sorts of sharp, jagged cast-offs which could cut me up nastily, even . . .

I grin weakly. I was going to say, *even kill me.* But I'm dead already. It's easy to forget when I'm walking around, thinking the way I always did. But I'm a corpse. No heart – that was ripped out of my chest – and no other properly functioning organs except for my brain, which for some reason keeps ticking over. If I misjudge my jump and a pole pierces my stomach and drives through my lungs, what of it? I'll just prise myself free and carry on my merry way. It will hurt, sure, but it's nothing to be scared of.

I back up, spread my arms for balance, then race

forward and jump. I expect to come up short, or to just make the edge of the roof. But to my shock I overshoot it by three or four metres and come crashing back to earth with a startled shriek. My fall is broken by a stack of dishwashers, which scatter and shatter beneath the weight of my body.

Cursing, I pick myself up and glare at the shed. I didn't do much leaping around when I was captive underground. It seems the muscles in my legs are stronger than they were in life. I think I might have just broken the women's long-jump record. B Smith — Olympic athlete!

I climb on to the roof of the shed and jump to the next set of cars, putting less effort into the leap this time. I still sail over my target, but only by a metre. Next time I judge it right and land on top of an old Datsun, a short hop away from the gate.

I stare around uneasily before getting down. I'm expecting soldiers to spill out of the sheds, guns blazing. But I appear to be all alone in the yard.

At the gate I pause again. It's a simple wire gate and it isn't locked. But maybe it's electrified. I stick out a wary hand and nudge the wire with one of the bones jutting out of my fingertips. The gate swings open a crack. Nothing else happens.

One last glance over my shoulder. Then I shrug.

'Sod it,' I mutter and let myself out, slipping from the scrapyard into the silent, solemn city beyond.

TWO

The area outside the scrapyard is deserted. Old boarded-up houses, derelict for years. Faded signs over stores or factories which closed for business long before I was born. The only thing that looks halfway recent is the graffiti, but there's not even much of that, despite the fact that this place boasts all the blank walls a graffiti artist could dream of. It feels like a dead zone, an area which nobody lived in or visited any time in living memory.

I stagger along a narrow, gloomy street, seeking the shade at the side. The worst of the itching dies away once I get out of the sunlight. My eyes stop stinging too. The irritation's still there but it's bearable now.

Halfway up the street, the stabbing pain in my stomach comes again and I fall to my knees, dry-heaving, whining like a dying dog. I bare my unnaturally long, sharp teeth and thump the side of my head with my hand, trying to knock my senses back into place.

The pain increases and I roll over. I bang into a wall and punch it hard, tearing the skin on my knuckles. That would have brought tears to my eyes if all my tear ducts hadn't dried up when I died.

My back arches and my mouth widens. I stare at the sky with horror, thinking I'll never look at it again this way, as a person capable of thought. In another few seconds I'll be a brainless zombie, a shadow of a girl, lost to the world forever.

But to my relief the pain passes and again I'm able to force myself to my feet, mind intact. I chuckle weakly at my lucky escape. But even as I'm chuckling, I know I must have used up all nine of my lives by this stage. I can't survive another dizzying attack like that. I'm nearing the end. Even the dead have their limits.

I stumble forward, reeling like a drunk. My legs don't want to support me and I almost go down, but I manage to keep my balance. Coming to the end of the street, I grab a lamp post and swing out into a road.

Several cars are parked along the pavement and a few have been stranded in the middle of the road. One has overturned. The windows are all smashed in and bones line the asphalt around it.

The sun is blinding again now that I've left the gloom. I hurry to the nearest car in search of shelter. When I get there, I find two people lying on the back seat. Both boast a series of bite marks and scratches, each one of which is lined with a light green moss.

The zombies raise their heads and growl warningly. This is their turf and they don't want to share it with me. Fair enough. I don't really want to bed down with them either.

I lurch to the next car but that's occupied too, this time by a fat zombie who is missing his jaw — it was either ripped off when he was killed, or torn from him later. He looks comical and creepy at the same time.

The third car is empty and I start to crawl in out of the light, to rest in the shade and wait for my senses to crumble. To all intents and purposes, this car will serve as my tomb, the place where B Smith gave up the ghost and became a true member of the walking dead.

But just as I'm bidding farewell to the world of the conscious, my nostrils twitch. Pausing, I pull back and sniff the air. My taste buds haven't been worth a damn since I returned to life, but my sense of smell is stronger than ever. I've caught a whiff of something familiar, something which I was eating for a long time under-ground without knowing what it was.

Three cars further down the road is a Skoda, the source of the tantalising scent. As weary as I am and as agonising as it is, I force myself on, focusing on the Skoda and the sweet, sweet smell.

My legs give out before I get to the car, but I don't let that stop me. Digging my finger bones into the asphalt, I drag myself along, crawling on my belly like a worm, baking in the sun, half-blind, itching like mad, brain shutting down. Every part of me wants to give up and die, but the scent lures me on, and soon I'm hauling myself into the Skoda through the front passenger door.

The driver is still held in place by her seat belt, but is lying slumped sideways. Most of her flesh has been torn from her bones, and her head has been split open, her brains scooped out and gobbled up by the zombies who caught her as she was trying to flee. She's not entirely fresh but she's not rotting either. She must have been killed quite recently.

I should feel sympathy for the woman and curiosity about how she survived this long and where she was headed when she was attacked. But right now all I'm concerned about is that those who fed on her didn't scrape her dry. Bits of brain have been left behind. Slivers are stuck to her scalp and meatier chunks rest inside the hollow of her skull.

Like a monstrous baby taking to the teat, I latch on to the shattered bones and suck tendrils of brain from them. I run my tongue the whole way round the rim, not caring about the fact that it's disgusting, that I'm behaving like an animal. In fact I'm ecstatic, getting an unbelievable buzz from the grey scraps, feeling myself

strengthen as I suck, knowing I can keep the senseless beast inside me at bay for a while longer.

When I've sucked the bones dry, I pull back a touch, wipe my lips, then steel myself for what I have to do next. 'For what I am about to receive ...' I mutter, trying to make a sick joke out of the even sicker deed.

Then I stick my fingers into the dead woman's head, scoop out every bit of brain that I can find, and stuff myself like a cannibal at Christmas.

THREE

Once I'm done dining, I lean out of the car and force myself to vomit. If I keep food inside my system, it will rot and attract insects. I've no wish to become a sanctuary for London's creepy-crawlies.

I pull back inside and shelter from the sunlight as best I can, staring glumly at the ceiling of the car, thinking about the underground complex, Rage killing Dr Cerveris and leaving us to our own devices, poor Mark being eaten, the zom heads being burnt alive. What a horrible, pointless mess, the whole bloody lot of it.

The road outside is deserted. Nobody moves. The zombies are lying low, hiding from the sun like me.

I'm itching all over. I scratch gently, careful not to slice through my skin with the bones sticking out of my fingers. I catch sight of my injured knuckles and peel some of the ruined flesh away from them. The damage isn't bad but I'm probably stuck with the wound for life. (Or whatever passes for life these days.) The hole in my chest where my heart was ripped out hasn't healed fully, so I don't think this will either. I'm dead. Your body doesn't regenerate when you're a zombie.

Still, I won't have to bear the open scars too much longer. Normal zombies can last as long as an ordinary person. Those of us who recover our senses aren't so lucky. Dr Cerveris told me that the brains of revitaliseds start to decompose once they fire up again. I've got a year, maybe eighteen months, then I'm toast.

The day passes slowly. I think about the past, where Mum and Dad might be now, if they're alive, dead or wandering the streets of London as zombies. I recall the attack on my school. I wonder about the freaky clown and his mutants, why they tore through the compound, slaughtering all in sight, but freeing the zombies.

I wish I could sleep and kill some time that way, but the dead can't snooze. We're denied almost all of the pleasures of the flesh. The only thing we can still enjoy is food — as long as it's brains.

'You had it easy,' I tell the corpse on the front seat, moving into the back as the sun swings round. 'A couple of minutes of terror and pain, then it was all over. You probably didn't think you were one of the lucky ones as your skull was being clawed open, but trust me, you were.'

The woman doesn't respond, but I go on speaking to her anyway, telling her my story, my thoughts, my regrets, my fears. It's the first time I've talked about my feelings since I recovered consciousness. There was nobody in the compound I could confide in. Mark was the closest I had to a friend, but I couldn't trust him completely. For all I knew he was working for the doctors, a plant. And in fact he was, only he didn't know about it until it was too late.

The dead are the best listeners in the world. The corpse takes it all in, never interrupts, doesn't criticise me, lets me waffle on for as long as I like.

Finally the sun dips and night falls on London. I feel nervous as I slide out of the car. I've no idea what to expect. The soldiers and scientists told me nothing about the outside world. I don't know how much damage the zombies caused when they went wild, or if the living managed to suppress them. By what I've seen on this road – the lack of activity, the silence, the zombies sheltering in deserted cars – I assume the worst. But I won't know for sure until I explore some more.

The other zombies come out as I do, free to move around without irritation now that the sun has set. They don't shuffle like movie zombies – they walk almost as freely as when they were alive – but you couldn't mistake them for the living. Their eyes are glassed over, bones stick out of their fingers and toes, their teeth are too big for their mouths, they sniff the air like dogs.

The fat guy I saw earlier gets a whiff of me and moves in closer, head twitching as he sniffs and listens.

I let him come as close as he likes, curious to see what he'll do, if he can tell that I'm different to him.

Something must register inside his chaotic mess of a brain, telling him I'm not entirely the same, because he circles me warily, studying me with his cold, dead eyes.

'Take it easy, boss,' I grunt, pulling up my T-shirt to reveal the hole in my chest. 'I'm one of you, honest I am.'

The zombie growls when he hears me talking, then frowns when he spots the hole where my heart once rested. He peers into it for ages, as if he thinks it might be a trick. Then he turns away and goes looking for dinner elsewhere.

'We accept you, gooble-gobble ...' I murmur, remembering something Tiberius used to say. Then I press on, leaving my temporary shelter behind, to find out if London truly has become a city of the dead.

FOUR

The streets are mostly deserted and the only people I glimpse are zombies. They seem to be drifting aimlessly, sniffing the air, looking for living humans to feed on. Many groan or whine, scratching at their stomachs or heads, suffering hunger pangs. Some have accidentally clawed through to their guts or poked an eye out. They're pitiful beasts in this sorry state. They'd be better off properly dead, no doubt about it.

Lots of zombies stop me as I draw close. They can tell I'm not exactly the same as them, maybe by my scent or the way I move. In almost every case, their face lights up with excitement, then creases with doubt, then returns to blankness once they realise I'm dead like they are.

The reviveds become a nuisance after a while. If I try to push on without stopping to be examined, they get angry and snap at me. I'm pretty sure I could take any one of them in a fight – it shouldn't be too difficult to outwit a brain-dead zombie – but I don't want to spend the whole night scrapping. It's easier to stand still, let them give me the once-over, then move on when they lose interest.

To clarify my situation, I rip a hole in my T-shirt to expose the left half of my chest. That speeds things up a bit, but some still stop me to make absolutely sure I'm not one of the living. With all the interruptions, I make little headway. It's been about a couple of hours since I left the car, but I haven't gone far.

I spot a newsagent's and let myself in. It's dusty. Shelves have been knocked down, broken bottles litter the floor, the glass in a drinks cabinet has been shattered. There are a few newspapers on the counter, all dated the day of the zombie attacks, the world's last normal day. The cash register is open, notes lying undisturbed inside it. I guess money doesn't matter much any more.

The electricity is off but I can see fairly clearly. My eyes work well in the dark, better than they do in strong light.

I find a large *A to Z* and take it outside. I look for a street sign, then do a quick check in the book. I'm in the East End. I don't know this area well, but I'm not far from more familiar territory. It's probably pointless, but with nowhere else to head for, I figure I might as well go home. I doubt I'll find anyone there, but at least I'll be in more comforting surroundings.

I replace the *A to Z* with a smaller version and stick it in the back of my jeans. Then I set off in a north-west direction, picking my way through the streets, stopping whenever I'm challenged by one of the roaming dead.

I endure the stop-start process for another hour before I get sick of it. It'll take forever if I keep going like this. There has to be a better way and I think I know what it is. I could try a motorbike or car, of course, but I never learnt to drive, and anyway, the roads are cluttered with crashed vehicles.

I find a street packed with shops and go on a scouting mission. First I slip into a chemist's and hunt for eye drops. My eyes don't produce tears now, so I need to keep moistening them or they'll dry out and my vision will worsen. Once I've doused them, I load a bag with several bottles and look around, wondering if I need anything else. I think about bandaging over the hole in my chest, but it's not a medical necessity – apart from the green moss, I haven't seen any signs of infection – and besides, the open hole makes it easier for the walking dead to identify me as one of their own.

I move on and spot a hardware store. I spend a bit longer in this shop, testing a variety of tools, looking for weapons in case I have to fight at any point. The zombies haven't bothered me so far, but I can't rely on them leaving me alone forever. I know from the tests underground that they'll attack revitaliseds if they feel threatened. I don't plan on antagonising anyone, but sometimes things can just kick off. Better to be safe than sorry.

I settle on a hammer, a couple of screwdrivers and a chisel. Light, easy to carry and use, effective. I spend a long time among the drills, playing around with them, wincing at the shriek they make – my sense of hearing is much better than it was when I was alive – but loving their sheer ferocity. It would be cool to become a drill-packing zombie, but the bulky machines aren't practical, so in the end, reluctantly, I leave them behind.

A file, on the other hand, is vital, and I spend even longer testing out the goods in that section. My teeth are constantly growing and need to be filed back every day or two. Otherwise they'll fill my mouth and I won't be able to speak. When I find a file that does the job, I give all of my teeth a thorough going-over, then stick it in my bag, along with replacements, and mosey on.

Next up, a large department store. Zombies are patrolling the aisles, checking behind clothes racks, looking for any juicy humans they might have missed. They keep mistaking mannequins for living people. They jump on them, growling and howling, then realise their mistake and trudge away sullenly. I get a good laugh out of that, but lose interest after the seventh or eighth time and crack on.

I browse the racks, looking for clean jeans, a new T-shirt and a long-sleeved, heavy jumper. I tear a hole through the jumper and T-shirt to show the cavity in my chest, then pick up gloves and a nice leather jacket, one of the most expensive in the store. I dress in the middle of the shop, not bothering with the changing rooms. The zombies don't take any notice of me as I strip off. They're not interested in nudity, only brains.

I try on shoes once I'm comfortable in the clothes, but can't easily slip them on because of the bones poking out of my toes. Finally I grab a few pairs of socks and jam them over my feet, letting the bones stick out through the ends.

A good hat is the next item on my shopping list. I don't find anything that I like in the women's section, so I head to the men's department and spot an Australian cork hat. Once I've pulled off the corks and string, it's perfect — with its wide brim, it will shade my face and neck.

'G'day, mate,' I drawl in a terrible Australian accent,

studying myself in a mirror. 'Looking good, sport.' I try to wink at my reflection, forgetting again that my eyelids don't work. I scowl, then laugh at my foolishness. 'No worries!'

I make my final stop by one of the sales desks, where sunglasses lie scattered across the floor. I root through and find a few which fit me and which I don't mind the look of. When I'm happy with my choices, I put three pairs in my bag and clip the other pair on to the neck of my jumper.

All sorted, I grab some magazines, return to the windows at the front of the store and lie down. I spend the rest of the night reading about showbiz stars who will never glitter again now that the world has gone to hell, glancing up every so often to watch the occasional zombie prowl past outside.

When dawn breaks and the streets clear, I get up, toss the magazines aside, slip on my glasses and hat, pull on my gloves and step out into the brightening day. My eyes tighten behind the shades but gradually adjust. They're not as sharp as they were in the darkness, but protected by the dark glasses, I can see OK.

I move into the middle of the road and stand bathed by the rays of the sun, to test whether or not they irritate me through the covering of my clothes. They do to an extent, and the itching starts again, but it's nowhere near as bad as it was. I can live with it, so to speak.

'Right,' I snap. 'The day is mine.'

And off I set through the empty streets, claiming them as my own. B Smith — queen of the city!

FIVE

In all honesty, it's not much of a city to be queen of. I used to think that London was one of the most exciting places in the world, always buzzing, always something going on. Now it's like walking through the world's biggest graveyard, and an ugly, messy one at that.

The battle between the living and the dead must have been apocalyptic. There are signs of chaos everywhere, broken windows, crashed cars, corpses left to rot outdoors. Many houses and shops are burnt out and fires still smoulder in some of them. In other places pipes have burst and streets are flooded.

There are bloodstains everywhere and lots of dried pools of vomit. The reviveds might not be as mentally clued-up as I am, but it looks like they figured out the vomiting part easily enough. I guess even the mostly senseless dead get a shiver at the notion of playing host to a brood of worms, maggots and the like.

The stench isn't as bad as I thought it would be, but it's fairly gross all the same, especially since my nose is more sensitive than it once was.

Birds, rats and insects are feasting on the vomit, blood and rotting flesh. They're enjoying the run of the city now that the zombies have withdrawn for the day. The more alert creatures scatter as soon as they spot me, the birds taking to the air, the rats vanishing down the nearest hole. Only the insects ignore me and go about their business uninterrupted.

The electricity supply varies from street to street. In some it's been cut off and every house is dead. In others it's as strong as ever, lights are on, static crackles from radios, TV sets flicker in shop windows. I consider checking the channels, to find out if anyone is alive and broadcasting, but I can do that later.

I want to continue exploring on foot first, not waste the tranquillity of the daylight. I can channel-surf tonight when the zombies come out in force and I hole up.

I come to a butcher's shop, pause and stick my head inside. Slabs of dried-out meat lie rotting everywhere. A few scavenging flies crawl across the withered cuts, searching for bits that are still edible, but I think they'll struggle.

A pig's carcass hangs upside down from a hook. Its head has been clawed open. I stare at it thoughtfully. I'm guessing that a zombie ripped out the brain, which maybe means we can thrive on animal brains too. I thought only human brains would keep us going, but it's good news if we can absorb nutrients from animals as well — I'd much rather scoop clean the inside of a pig's head than a human's.

This might be why I haven't seen any larger creatures. With humanity out of the way, wild dogs and cats should have the run of the streets. But so far I've seen nothing but rats, birds and smaller specimens. Maybe the zombies killed and ate the brains of larger animals, and all of London's pets have either been butchered or scared off.

I'll have to swing by London Zoo at some point. It's probably been cleaned out already – or the animals will most likely have died of starvation – but maybe I'll be able to gain access to areas off-limits to normal zombies. The good thing about having a working brain is that you can read maps and search for keys to unlock doors, simple tasks which are beyond most of the undead.

As I turn away from the pig, I notice a small red z painted on the frame of the door, a tiny arrow just beneath it. I frown, trying to remember where I've seen something like that before. Then I recall Mr Dowling daubing my cheek with a mark just like this one.

I glance around nervously. Have the clown and his mutants been here? Might they be watching me now? Mr Dowling freaked me out big time, especially when he opened his lips and dropped a stream of living spiders over me. I don't want to hang around and risk another run-in with him.

Hurrying from the shop, I come to a set of traffic

lights. The electricity is working here and the lights are operating as normal. The red man is illuminated and I automatically stop, waiting for the light to change to green.

After a few seconds, I squint at the light, look left, then right. Nothing moves.

'Of course not,' I grimace. 'There's no traffic because everyone's dead. You're a bloody moron, B.'

I chuckle at my stupidity. Stopping for a traffic light in a city of the dead! I'm glad none of my friends lived to see that. Ignoring the red light, I step out into the road. I'm not far from my old neighbourhood. Another hour, maybe a bit more, and I'll be back on –

An engine roars into life. My head snaps round and I spot a car tearing towards me. It had been parked nearby. I'd seen people moving around inside, but figured they were zombies sheltering from the sun.

I figured wrong.

Before I can withdraw to the safety of the pavement, the driver turns on his headlights and I'm momentarily blinded, even wearing the sunglasses. Wincing,

I turn my head away and shake it wildly, disoriented and in pain.

Then the car smashes into me and knocks me flying through the air, far down the middle of the road, which up until a few seconds ago seemed just as dead and unthreatening as any other in this ghost city of the damned.

SIX

SIX

I hit the ground hard and slide for a few metres before coming to a stunned stop. Shaking my head, I woozily get to my feet. No bones seem to be broken, but my elbows have been badly grazed and the back of my head is throbbing. I run a hand over my scalp. Lots of torn flesh but it doesn't feel too serious. The jacket and clothes I picked up earlier are ripped to shreds, but all things considered it could have been a lot worse.

Then the doors of the car open and as four men step

out, I realise it's far too soon to be judging this a lucky escape.

The men are dressed in combats and black boots. Each totes a rifle and I spot smaller guns and hunting knives strapped to their legs and chests. They're smiling and laughing, not looking in the least afraid.

'She's up,' one of the men says. 'You must be losing your touch, Coley.'

'I'm not losing anything,' the man called Coley snaps. 'I was only doing about thirty when I hit her. Didn't want to finish her off too soon. Essex, you want first shot?'

'Don't mind if I do,' the man on my far left says and raises his rifle.

I dive for cover behind a nearby car as he fires. He curses and fires again, but only hits one of the wheels.

'You missed,' Coley hoots.

'No fair!' Essex shouts. 'They're not supposed to hide.'

'Not all of them stand still,' one of the other men says, and this guy speaks in a thick American accent. 'The survival instinct is still alive in some. Looks like we might have a real hunt on our hands, gentlemen.'

'You want to deal with her, Barnes?' Coley asks.

'No,' the American says. 'Let's give Tag a shot first. This is what we brought them along for.'

'What do I do?' the fourth man asks. He sounds nervous.

'Edge over to your right,' Barnes says, and I hear him creeping around to my left. 'I'll flush her out. As soon as she –'

I don't wait for him to give more orders. Keeping low, I race back towards the butcher's shop, catching the men by surprise. A couple yell with alarm and fire wildly. Bullets scream past but I keep going.

I'm close to the shop when one of the men hits the window with a bullet and it shatters. As glass sprays everywhere, I fling myself through the hole and roll across the counter before dropping to the floor and taking cover.

'Hellfire!' Essex shouts. 'Did you see that?'

'Careful, boys,' Barnes drawls. 'We've got a live one here. Relatively speaking.'

'How do you want to play this?' Coley asks. He sounds excited.

'That depends on these two,' the American says. 'Do you want to go in after her and risk the thrill of a close encounter, or would you rather we smoked her out?'

As they discuss tactics, I raise my head, get a fix on them, then scout around and pick up a hefty butcher's knife. This is why I came back here rather than flee down the road. I was a target out there, the tools I picked up earlier no use against a group of guys with guns. I hate being trapped like this, but at least I have a decent weapon now.

Shuffling backwards, I search for another way out. There's a door at the rear of the shop, but it's locked and I can't find the key. I hurl myself at the door, hoping to smash through, but it's made of metal and it holds. I only bounce off it, bruising my arm in the process.

'What's she doing?' I hear Tag cry.

'Maybe she's lost her head and is thrashing around,' Barnes says calmly. 'Or she might be trying to find another way out. Coley, swing round back and make sure she doesn't sneak away.'

'She wouldn't be smart enough to think of that,' Coley says.

'You'd be surprised,' Barnes grunts. 'Some are almost as cunning as they were in life.'

As Coley circles round, the American addresses the other pair. 'This is unusual but not unheard of. Some of these beasts are smarter than others. They recall routines and procedures in some dim corner of their foul, undead brain and act like they did when they were alive.'

'How dangerous are they?' Tag asks.

'All zombies are dangerous,' Barnes huffs.

'But if this one's more of a threat than most, shouldn't we back off and leave her be?'

'We're hunters,' Barnes says stiffly. 'We don't withdraw once we've engaged our prey. We have to see this through to the end. If you prefer, you can return to the car and wait for us there, but my advice is to stick together. Never forget that this is a city of the undead. There's safety in numbers. I can't protect you if you cut yourself off from the rest of us.'

'I didn't know it was going to be like this,' Tag grumbles.

'Quit whining,' Essex snarls. 'They told us it could turn nasty. We knew the risks coming in. This is all part of the fun, right, Barnes?'

'Sure,' Barnes says drily. '*Fun*. That's what we promised you guys and we won't let you down. Coley, you in place yet?'

'Got it covered,' Coley shouts.

'Then if you boys will give me a minute . . .'

There's a long pause. I peer over the counter, trying to see what they're up to, but Tag and Essex start firing as soon as they spot my head. Ducking again, I curse and grab another knife, determined not to go down without a fight and maybe take one or two of these bastards with me.

'Come on,' I whisper, gripping the knife tightly. 'Meet me on my own turf. Let's see how useful your rifles are up close.'

But the American is obviously thinking the same way I am, because even as I'm willing them to advance, he yells a warning to the others, 'Clear!'

A couple of seconds later a bottle comes flying through the window. There's a burning rag sticking out of the top of it. I don't know much about weapons, but I know a Molotov cocktail when I see one.

The bottle smashes into the wall and flames billow from it, scorching the shop, roasting the flies, blackening the scraps of meat. I don't wait to be engulfed by the fire. I started moving the instant I caught sight of the bottle flying over my head. As the glass explodes and flames roar around me, I launch myself over the counter and shoot through the window like a human bullet propelled from the heated chamber of the store.

Crashing back to earth, pain flares in my feet and I see that my socks are on fire. Yelping, I toss the knife aside and slap out the flames, then tear off the smouldering socks. I'm so concerned about my feet that I blank out everything else. It's only when I hear a soft clicking noise that I pause, look up and realise that the barrels of three rifles are pointed directly at my head.

SEVEN

Nobody says anything and nobody opens fire. The American is slightly in front of the others, studying me coolly, the mouth of his rifle trained on the centre of my forehead. The other two look less sure of themselves. I think of diving for the knife, but I'm afraid that if I move, their trigger fingers will tighten instinctively and that will be the end of me.

'She's smart for a dead bird, isn't she?' Coley remarks, sauntering back into view, rifle slung across his shoulder, grinning viciously. His hair is cut short like a soldier's and he's wearing a pair of designer sunglasses. 'Seems almost a shame to kill her.'

'It's not really killing, is it?' Tag frowns. He's a thin man with a Scottish accent. Long hair tied back in a ponytail. 'I mean, they're dead already, so it's not like we're murdering anyone, right?'

'Don't worry,' Barnes murmurs, never taking his eyes off me. 'This isn't a crime. Nobody will hold us accountable for what we do here. She looks like one of us but she isn't. She has less right to exist than an animal. It's elimination, not execution. Now, who wants to –'

'Screw you all!' I scream and every one of the men recoils with shock.

'Jesus!' Essex roars. 'She spoke! Did you hear that? She bloody *spoke!*'

'I heard,' Barnes growls. His dark brown eyes are hard. He's taller than the others, lean and muscular. He's the only one not wearing gloves. His black hair is shot through with streaks of grey and there's a bullet tucked behind his right ear.

'What the hell is she?' Coley asks. He doesn't look so relaxed now, and has trained his rifle on me too.

'I don't know,' Barnes says softly.

'Is she alive?' Tag asks.

'She can't be,' Essex snorts. 'Look at the hole in her chest.'

'But she spoke.'

'Maybe it was a reflex action,' Essex says.

'Reflex action my arse!' I shout and again they flinch. I push myself to my feet and glower at the astonished hunters. 'My name's Becky Smith. I'm a teenage girl. If you shoot me, you can bet a million pounds there are plenty of people out there who bloody *will* hold you accountable.'

Barnes blinks and lowers his rifle a fraction. 'Are you a zombie?'

'What does it look like?' I sniff, pointing a finger at the hole in my chest.

'Then how are you speaking?'

'Some of us can.'

'None that I've seen,' he counters.

I shrug. 'Maybe if you asked first and shot later ...'

'This is insane,' Coley mutters, circling me slowly, keeping well out of reach, nervously eyeing the bones sticking out of my fingers. 'Every zombie we've ever seen is a rabid, senseless beast. There can't be an in-between state.'

'Well, there is. I'm proof of that.'

'There are others like you?' Barnes asks.

'Yeah.' Then I recall Mr Dowling, the mutants, the flame-throwers. 'At least, there *were* . . .'

'Where are they?'

'I don't know. We were being kept underground. Most of the others were killed, maybe all of them. I got away but I think I'm the only one. The clown attacked and everything went crazy.'

I stop, aware that I'm making no sense.

'Who *kept* you?' Barnes asks.

'Soldiers. Scientists. They were studying us.'

'Soldiers?' Essex yelps. He looks around, edgy now. 'This sounds bad to me. If the military's involved . . .'

'We're not doing anything they'd disapprove of,' Coley says quickly. 'We're zombie hunters, that's all, helping clean up the mess.'

'But we're not supposed to be here,' Tag mumbles.

'Only because it's dangerous,' Coley reassures him. 'They tell people to keep away because they want to stop fools being killed or turned into zombies. But nobody's going to give professionals like us any grief for coming in and shooting some of the buggers. We're saving them a job.'

'Still,' Essex says, pointing his gun away from me, 'I think we should split. I don't want to be caught here by the army. They might mistake us for zombies and open fire from afar. I want to leave now.'

'We came here to hunt,' Coley snarls. 'You both begged to join us. We didn't force you.'

'I know,' Essex says stiffly. 'But now I want to stop. Tag?'

'Hell, yes.' He lowers his rifle.

'Bloody amateurs.' Coley spits with disgust, then cocks an eyebrow at Barnes. The American hasn't budged. 'What do we do?'

'If there are soldiers in the area, Tag and Essex are right, we need to get out of here. We're breaking the law. They might let us go with a slap on the wrist. Or they might shoot us dead. We'd be fools to risk it.'

'Fair enough,' Coley sighs. Lowering his rifle, he pulls a handgun and aims it at my face.

'What the hell!' I roar, throwing myself to the ground.

'Coley!' Barnes yells.

'What?' he frowns. 'She's a zombie. It doesn't matter whether she can talk or not. She's one of them.'

'One of the undead, definitely,' Barnes agrees, 'but partially one of the living too. I don't know how she can respond, but she's more than a walking corpse.'

Coley laughs cynically. 'Not much more. I say we kill her. One less zombie is always a good thing.'

He takes aim again.

'This is murder!' I howl. 'I can talk! I can think! I used to go to school!'

I don't know why I shouted that last line. It just popped out.

'Hush now,' Coley purrs. 'One little bullet and all your worries will be behind you.'

'Hold,' Barnes barks. 'We're hunters, not killers. We mop up the dead, we don't execute the living.'

'She's a zombie,' Coley protests.

'But unlike any other we've encountered. She can reason. She can plead for her life. We don't have the right to kill someone who understands what we're doing.'

'Not a some*one*,' Coley sneers. 'A some*thing*. And you might be going soft in your old age, but I'm not about to lose focus. These bastards killed the people I loved. I won't stop as long as they're active and I don't give a damn if they can talk or not.'

Coley cocks his gun. Tag and Essex gawp like children. Barnes goes on staring at me.

'She said her name is Becky Smith,' Barnes says softly.

'I heard.' Coley shrugs. 'I don't care.'

'Have you ever killed something that could tell you its name?' Barnes presses.

'As it happens, yes,' Coley says. 'That didn't stop me then and it sure as hell won't stop me now. She's a bloody zombie! They're the bad guys, remember?'

'I don't know about good and I don't know about bad,' Barnes replies softly. 'Until a few minutes ago all that mattered to me was the living and the undead. I thought the world had been divided neatly along those lines and I operated accordingly. Now I see it's not so simple. I can't kill this girl. Even though she's missing a heart, she's too much like a real person.'

Coley stiffens. 'Are you saying you'll stop me if I try to shoot her?'

Barnes considers that. I start to smile. Then he says, 'No,' and my smile fades away to nothing.

Coley grins and takes final aim.

'I don't have the right to stop you shooting her,' Barnes adds. 'You're a free agent, I'm not your boss, you're not answerable to me. And maybe you're right — maybe she is a monster, and we have every right to cull her like a rabid hound. But if you kill her, I'll put a bullet through each of your kneecaps and leave you here for the other zombies to pick apart come night.'

Coley does a double take. Barnes's expression doesn't change. If he's bluffing, he's got a first-rate poker face.

'You'd do that to me?' Coley asks softly. 'After all we've been through these last six months?'

'I'd have to,' Barnes says. 'In my view that would be the only appropriate response. If you feel you have to kill this girl, I won't stop you. But be aware of the consequences.'

'You'd choose a zombie over a friend?' Coley snarls.

'You're no friend of mine, any more than I'm a friend of yours.' Barnes smiles icily. 'We're just a couple of guys who hunt together.'

Coley weighs up his options. I can tell he'd love to put a bullet through Barnes's head almost as much as he wants to put one through mine. But the American has a lethal air about him. He's not someone you go up against lightly.

'Have it your way,' Coley finally snarls, holstering his gun. He heads for the car, not looking at any of the others.

'Head on back, boys,' Barnes says, nodding at Tag and Essex. In a daze they follow Coley to the vehicle and get in. Coley fires up the engine and revs it angrily. For a moment I think he plans to mow down the American. But Barnes never gives any indication that he's worried. And although the car rumbles forward a metre or so, Coley doesn't push things any further.

'You've had a lucky escape today,' Barnes says.

'Yes,' I gulp. 'Thank you.'

'In this city, you'd better hope you stay lucky,' he mutters, then backs up, keeping his rifle trained on me the whole way, until he gets into the car. As soon as the door slams shut, the car squeals past. The last thing I see of the hunters is an angry-looking Coley giving me the finger.

Then the car turns a corner and is gone, leaving me lying alone in the road, still trembling at my narrow escape.

EIGHT

I drag myself through the streets, limping, bruised, the flesh torn to shreds on my elbows and at the back of my head. I don't think any bones are broken, though I can't be certain. The pain isn't as bad as it would be if I was alive, but it's pretty damn excruciating.

I recall the look of hatred in Coley's eyes as I stumble along. Oddly enough, I don't blame him for wanting to kill me. I probably had that same look when I first saw a zombie. We're monsters, plain and simple. The dead can, by definition, have no automatic right to life.

I make slower progress than before, hampered by my injuries. It's dusk before I turn into the street where I used to live. Some of the keener or hungrier zombies have already come out of hiding and are on patrol. A few stop and sniff me as I pass, losing interest when they realise I'm more like them than one of the living.

Finally I come to the block of flats where I grew up. I can see from here that our front door is open. We have electricity in this area but no lights are on inside. It doesn't look like anyone's home. Which is a good thing. My greatest fear as I drew closer was that I'd find Mum, eyes glassed over, human flesh stuck between her teeth, lost to me forever in a state worse than death. (I'm not so worried about Dad, as I'm pretty certain he made it out alive. He has the luck of the devil.) I'm not sure what I'd do if I found her and she was a zombie. I'd want to kill her, to end her suffering, but I don't think that I could.

I spot a few familiar faces on the street, neighbours from a past that seems a thousand years removed. Nobody that I really cared about though. Ignoring them, I crawl up the three flights of stairs – as I pass a giant arse which was spray-painted on the wall, I slap it for luck and grin fleetingly at the memory of happier times – and limp along the landing, then step inside what used to be my home and shut the door on the outside world.

The flat smells musty. The heating hasn't been turned on for months and none of the windows are open. Most of the doors are closed – a habit of Mum's, she couldn't bear an open door – so the rooms are stuffy.

I do a tour of the flat, making sure I'm alone. No bloodstains anywhere, which is a promising sign. No zombies lying in any dark corners either, which is even better. Maybe Mum made it out after all. Perhaps Dad came for her after I split from him at school, took her somewhere safe. They could be living the high life on some paradise island now.

'Yeah,' I sneer at myself. 'Dream on!'

I get a pang in my chest where my heart should be when I look into their bedroom. Some of Mum's clothes are laid across the bed, three different sets. She was obviously choosing what to wear that night when the world went to hell. I can picture her standing here, staring at the clothes, trying to decide. Then ...

What? Killed by a zombie? Turned into one of the living dead? Taken off to some mystical Shangri-La by her racist, wife-beating knight in shining armour?

I don't know. All I know for sure is that she never made a final choice. The clothes stayed here, strewn across the bed, never to be worn again.

'I miss you, Mum,' I moan and wait for tears to come. But of course they don't. They can't. So in the end I close the door and go to check my own room.

It looks smaller than I remembered, dark and poky. I turn on the light, but that just makes it seem even more claustrophobic, full of ominous shadows. I gaze round. My bed looks the same as it always did, crumpled black sheets, the indent of my head on the pillow. No bookshelves or posters. I didn't believe in cluttering up my room. I liked my space, me.

I spot my iPod lying on the table next to my bed. I pick it up and smile softly. I left it charging the morning I set off to school for the last time, so it's warm to the touch. I scroll through a couple of my playlists, select a song at random and stick my headphones on. I yelp and immediately turn down the volume. It's easy to forget how good my sense of hearing is. Back then I used to set the volume up almost to maximum. If I did that now, I'd deafen myself.

I let the song play to its end, then lay down the iPod and step out of the room. I'd been looking forward to settling in here again, lying on my old bed and staring at the patch of ceiling which I knew so well. But now that I've seen it, I've gone off the idea. Instead I head back to Mum and Dad's room, sweep the clothes from the bed (I never was overly sentimental), lie back and cross my legs.

'Night night,' I murmur after a few minutes, then turn on my side. I can't sleep, not since I was killed, but there's no harm in pretending every once in a while, is there?

NINE

I spend several days in the flat, maybe even a couple of weeks. Hard to tell for sure — one monotonous day blends into another and I lose track after a while. I only leave three times, to feed. On each occasion, being new to the whole brain-eating game, I track other zombies. They shuffle around the streets, sniffing like pigs in search of truffles. Often they go for hours without finding anything, but in the end they usually manage to track down an old corpse with some scraps of brain still left in its head.

I expected the zombies to fight over the meagre

morsels, but they feed politely, taking turns, waiting patiently while others gorge themselves. Sometimes they get a bit overeager and try to butt in, but always pull back if the feasting creature growls warningly at them.

I hate having to feed on the dried-up, rubbery bits of brain, but it's eat or lose my mental faculties completely. I keep looking for animals, but I still haven't seen any, apart from the birds and rats. I've eaten the brains of a few dead crows and rodents, and even caught a live rat once — I think it must have been sick or lame, because it couldn't run very fast. But they haven't made any real difference. Too small. I'd need to tuck into a dog or cat's brain to find out if it could do the job that a human's does for me.

The rest of the time I hole up in the flat, recovering. My wounds don't heal, but the dull ache fades from my bones and my thick, jelly-like blood combines with the green moss to form thin, wispy scabs around the scrapes. After a few days, I'm good as new (well, as close to it as a zombie can ever be), but I make no move to leave. I can't think of anywhere better to go.

I turned on the lights the first night, when I got tired of lying on the bed, but they attracted curious zombies, so I've sat in the dark since then. A few zombies wander in every so often – I've left the front door open, since one of them nearly broke it down when it heard someone at home and couldn't get in – but they slip out once they've satisfied themselves that my brain's of no use to them.

I check the TV every day but it produces nothing but static. The radio, on the other hand, is still going strong. I never used to listen to the radio – *so* twentieth century! – but Mum always had it playing in the background when she was cooking, ironing, etc.

There are far less channels than before. One for official state news, which plays all the time, run by whatever remains of our government and civil service, plus a few independents which broadcast sporadically.

The state reporters give the impression that the military have everything in hand, that they're restoring order, people shouldn't panic, it's all going to work out fine. The independents give more of a sense of the chaos that the world is experiencing. Some of them are critical of the soldiers, claiming they've been opening fire wildly in certain areas, killing the living as well as the dead. A few drop dark hints that the military staged the zombie coup and are eliminating anyone they don't approve of.

I don't pay too much attention to the politics of specific broadcasters. I'm not interested in any particular pundit's opinion. I just want to get to grips with as many cold, hard facts as I can. By switching between the various channels, and filtering out the positive spin of the state channel and the manic gloom of the independents, I fill in a lot of the blanks and get up to speed with what's been going on in the world since my heart was ripped out all those months ago.

Zombies launched simultaneous attacks in most major cities. New York, Tokyo, Moscow, Sydney, Berlin, Johannesburg and scores more, torn apart by the living dead, ruined graveyards of the grand cities they used to be.

The undead spread swiftly. They were almost impossible to stop. Armies everywhere opposed them, but all it needed was for one zombie to infect a couple of soldiers, and soon they were fighting among themselves, forced to break ranks and retreat. Estimates of the numbers lost to the hordes of the walking dead vary wildly, but most reporters agree that it's probably somewhere between four and five billion.

I have to repeat that slowly to myself the first time I hear it, and even then I can't really comprehend it. Four or five *billion*, most of the world's population, slaughtered or reduced to the status of reanimated corpses. How's this planet ever supposed to recover from that?

Nobody knows where the zombies came from, how the disease manifested itself so swiftly, so globally. And, in truth, nobody's overly concerned. Right now their first priority is survival.

When the attacks started, many small islands were spared. Survivors flocked to those on planes and boats. At first the residents accepted everyone. But then a few islands fell when boats docked or planes set down and zombies streamed out of them, having sneaked aboard. After that, the locals in other places began implementing security checks and setting up quarantine zones, opening fire on anyone who tried to bypass the process.

On the mainland continents, millions of people who can't get to the islands have established fortresses wherever they can. In some cases they've barricaded themselves into apartment complexes, prisons, schools or shopping malls.

Even though their forces have been severely depleted, the armies of the world are the sole governors of society now. Most politicians were wiped out in the first wave of attacks, and those who survived no longer have any real clout. It's martial law wherever you turn.

The troops in the UK have been busy reclaiming lost ground from the zombies. They've converted a series of towns and villages across the country into fortified barracks, building huge walls around them, including areas of open fields within the fortifications so that they can cultivate the land and live off what they grow.

The reporters on the state channel are proud of the army's sterling work and every news bulletin includes reports from some of the reclaimed towns, focusing on the resilience of the people living and working there, their struggle to survive, the way they're doing all that they can to rebuild normal lives for themselves.

The independents are more scathing. They say that residents are treated like cattle, forced to do whatever the soldiers tell them. If they resist, aerial units are sent to blow holes in their defences, to let zombies stream through freely.

I'm not convinced by the wilder reports, but in this zombie-plagued new world, who knows for sure? I keep an open mind, filing everything away.

The army's ultimate aim is to push the zombies back, section them off, then wipe them out. But that will take time. At the moment they're not equipped to engage in a full-on war with the undead. As stern generals keep explaining, their current focus must be on the three Rs — Reclaim, Recruit, Recover. Reclaim towns, recruit more survivors, recover their strength. *Then* they can let rip.

It's terrifying at first, thinking of humanity reduced to this, living off scraps, penned into grimy hovels, under constant siege by their former colleagues and relatives, knowing that all it takes is a single breach – one lone zombie in the mix – for everything they've worked so hard for to come crashing down around them.

But after a while, I get used to it. This is the norm now. You can only be shocked by a thing for so long before it starts to lose its impact. Yeah, the world's a dark, terrible place, and it's horrible listening to stories of children eating their parents or mothers chowing down on their young. But, y'know, when all's said and done, you've got to get on with things.

I only keep following the news after the first few days because of one particular story. The army has been making rescue attempts recently. Lots of people are trapped in cities, even after so many months, lying low at night, foraging for food and drink in the daytime while the zombies are at rest.

The military announce a city a few days ahead of a planned mission, telling the people who are listening to get ready. Then, on the morning of the rescue, they declare a meeting point and fly in at an appointed time, usually the middle of the day when the sun is at its strongest. They aren't always able to rescue everyone who turns up, and sometimes zombies attack, cutting the evacuation short. But they've extracted hundreds of refugees and escorted them to secure settlements, and have vowed to carry on.

Things would be a lot easier if the phones worked, but as I found out early on when I tested ours, they're even deader than the zombies. All of the landlines are down and all of the mobile networks too. The internet is screwed as well. The only way the army can contact trapped survivors is through the news on the radio, but that's a one-way means of communication.

According to the reports, there have been a few rescues in London already. As the capital, it's been granted priority status. They did trial runs in some of the smaller cities first, but now they're hitting London regularly, a different part every time, so as to keep one step ahead of the zombies.

The walking dead aren't as senseless as they appear. They seem to remember lots of functions, such as how to open doors or operate lifts. They've adapted — if they see a car passing a certain spot at a certain time more than once, they can anticipate its reappearance and lie in wait for it.

But they don't seem to understand most of what is said to them. They react to certain tones of voice, recognising a variety of commands, the way a baby or a dog can. But they're not able to listen to a broadcast and pitch up at a scheduled meeting place in advance.

If the living are to win this war, it will only be because they can out-think their opponents. In every other respect the zombies are a superior force, far greater in number, able to fight without tiring, not needing food or drink to continue. They don't have any weapons, but their bodies are deadly enough, dis-eased missiles that are much more effective than a bomb dropped in the middle of a confined group of people.

There have been two missions to London while I've been listening, one in the north, one in the west. Both pick-up points were out of my way, so I stayed put and let them pass. But it's only a matter of time before they come to the East End or the City, and I'm determined to go along when a rescue is announced.

There have been no reports of revitaliseds on any of the radio programmes. The world doesn't seem to be aware of the existence of zombies like me. I'm not sure how the soldiers will react when I turn up, but I've got to try to tell them about the possible threat which revitaliseds pose.

I've been thinking about Rage a lot, the way he killed Dr Cerveris, his contempt for the living. If he survived and made it out of the complex, maybe he looks upon the zombies as his allies. It might amuse him to betray humanity. Perhaps there are others like him who've been mistreated by the living, wanting to get revenge and see them brought low.

I don't know if the soldiers will give me a chance to explain, if they'll offer me shelter in return for my help or shoot me the instant they set eyes on me. I suspect it might be the latter. But I've got to at least try to help, because I was one of the living once, and if I don't cling to that memory and honour it, all that's left for me is the monstrous, lonely, sub-existence of the dead.

TEN

The call finally comes late one evening. There's going to be a mission to Central London in three days — to make it clear, the reporter says that today is Sunday and the rescue will take place sometime on Wednesday. She's excited when she breaks the news. The other rescues in the capital have all been in the suburbs. This is the first time they've hit the centre. They think it might be the largest operation yet, so they're going to be sending more helicopters and troops than normal. But she tells people not to worry, this is just the first mission of many, so if you can't make it this time, stay low and wait for the next.

I head off first thing in the morning. It won't take me three days to walk to the West End, but I want to allow myself plenty of time to overcome any unexpected obstacles along the way, explore the area, find a resting place, maybe meet up with some of the survivors and convince them of my good intentions so that they can act as middlemen between me and the soldiers.

I pause in the doorway of the flat and glance back one last time, nostalgic, remembering Mum and Dad, the bad times as well as the good. And, being honest, there were more bad days than good. Dad was always too free with his fists. Mum and I were constantly walking on eggshells, afraid we'd say the wrong thing and set him off.

But you know what? I'd take them all back in an instant if they were offered, even the days when he beat us and drew blood and kicked us like dogs. He was a nasty sod, there's no denying that, but he was still my dad. I love him. I miss him. I can't help myself.

'I'll come looking for you,' I say aloud to the memories of the two people who mattered to me most. 'If I survive, and you're out there, I'll try to find you, to let you know I made it through, to help you if I can.'

There's no answer or sign that somewhere, somehow, they magically heard. Of course not. I'd have to be a right dozy cow to believe that they're sitting up in a far-off compound, frowning at the ghostly echo of my voice, whispering with awe, '*B?*'

'You're getting soft, girl,' I mutter, then slam the door shut and head on down the stairs, whistling dreadfully — I can't carry a tune these days, not now that my mouth is drier than a camel's arse.

I wind my way through the streets, heading west. I've never walked this stretch of London before. We always got a bus or the Tube if we were going up the West End, or a cab on occasions when Dad was feeling flush.

I replace my clothes and jacket as soon as I can, for full protection from the sun. I'm still wearing the

Australian hat. That should last me years if I don't lose it. Well, *would* last me years if I lived that long, but I've probably only got about a year and a half, max. Which means this might well prove to be a lifelong hat.

The streets are quiet. I spot zombies in the shade of shops and houses, or resting in abandoned cars or buses. They stare at me hungrily as I amble past. I always make sure I turn so that they can see the hole in my chest. If it wasn't so bright, they'd probably clamber out to make sure I wasn't trying to fool them, but they're reluctant to brave the glare of the day. They haven't thought of wearing sunglasses. They ain't bright sparks like me.

I'm excited to be on the move, to have a goal, even if it's one that could result in my execution. I never did much when I was alive, just hung out with my mates (most or all of them are probably dead now, but I try not to brood about that) or festered in my room. It wasn't a fascinating life by any standards. But it beat the hell out of being held prisoner underground, and the monotony of the last few weeks. I was going stir-crazy in that flat, but I only realise how bad things were now that I've left. You know you've been seriously climbing the walls if the thought of heading off on a suicide mission makes you feel happy!

I lose my way a couple of times, but don't bother checking the *A to Z*. It's a nice day, I'm enjoying the stroll, no zombies or hunters are hassling me, so what's the rush?

I come to a railway station. Lots of eerie-looking train carriages, windows smashed in many, bloodstains splashed across the metal and glass in more places than I can count. On one carriage I spot a large red z with an arrow underneath, pointing west. It looks like it was freshly sprayed — there's even a smell of paint in the air, or is that my imagination?

I swing a right past the station and follow the road round until I can cut through to Victoria Park. Mum used to bring me for walks up here at the weekend when I was younger. Dad came with us sometimes, but he'd always work himself up into a mood, muttering about all the foreigners on the loose.

He wouldn't mind it now. There's not a soul to be seen, black, brown or any other colour. Lots of corpses and bones but that's all. I've got the entire park to myself.

Well ... not quite. As I pad past the tennis courts and come to a few small ponds, I spot three skinny dogs lapping water from a pool.

I perk up when I clock the dogs and hurry towards them, calling out, 'Hey! Doggies! Here!' I make clicking sounds with my tongue.

The dogs react instantly, but not in the way I'd like. Without even looking at me, they take off, yapping fearfully. I race after them, shouting for them to come back, but they're faster than me and disappear from sight moments later. I come to a stop and swear, then kick the ground with anger.

A little later, walking through the park, I regret swearing. I can't blame the dogs for running. These past months must have been hellish for any animal trapped here. If zombies eat an animal's brain as readily as a human's, they'll have gone for every pet in the city. To survive, you'd have to learn to be sneaky, to only come out in the daytime, to avoid all contact with the two-legged creatures which were once so nice to you. I think even Dr Dolittle would have trouble getting animals to trust him these days.

I spend an hour or more in the park. My skin's itching from the sun, even protected by my heavy layers of clothes, but I press on, determined not to let that spoil the day for me. A pity there's nobody selling ice cream. I could murder a 99, even though I'd have to spit out almost every mouthful because I can't digest solids any more.

I keep hoping the dogs will show again, that they'll realise I mean them no harm, that I only crave their friendship, not their brains — as hungry as I get, I wouldn't kill a dog, any more than I'd kill a living person. I want them to slink forward, give me a closer once-over, learn to trust me. But no such luck. They've gone into hiding and I doubt they'll come here again any time soon.

Eventually I take a road leading west. There are dead zombies hanging from the street lamps, rotting in the sun. Each has been shot through the head. Many have been disembowelled or cut up with knives. Flies buzz around the stinking corpses. I pass them nervously, wondering if this was the work of hunters like Barnes and his posse.

I don't like the way that the corpses have been strung up. As vicious as the living dead are, they're not consciously evil, just slaves to their unnatural desires. I understand the need to kill the undead, but torturing and humiliating them serves no purpose. It's not like other zombies are going to look at them and have a change of heart. Being a zombie isn't a career choice. The reviveds don't have any control over what they do.

I turn left, then right on to Bethnal Green Road. One of Mum's best friends, Mary Byrne, lived around here. Her oldest son, Matt, was my age, and his brother Joe was just a bit younger. We used to play together when our mums hung out.

More zombies are strung up along the road ahead of me, but I'm not paying attention to them, trying to remember exactly where Mary lived. So it's a real shock, as I'm walking along, when one of the corpses kicks out at my head and makes a choked noise.

'Bloody hell!' I yell, falling over and scrabbling away.

The zombie goes on kicking and mewling, and I

realise I have nothing to fear. I get to my feet and study the writhing figure. It's a man. He's been stripped bare. His hands are tied behind his back and a noose around his neck connects to the lamp overhead. But the people who strung up the zombies left this one alive, either for sport or because they were scared off before they could finish the job.

The man's flesh is a nasty red colour, where he's been burnt by the sun. His eyes are sickly white orbs. He snarls angrily and kicks out furiously at the world. No telling how long he's been up there, but by the state of his eyes, I'd say it's been a good while.

I should press on but I can't. This guy means nothing to me but I can't leave him like this. I wouldn't do this to anyone, even a savage killer, as he doubtless would become if given his freedom and a human target.

'Hold on, sunshine,' I tell him. 'I'll find a ladder and come free you.'

The zombie screeches hoarsely, limited by the rope around his throat.

'Be patient,' I snap. 'I won't be long. Just give me a few minutes to go search for . . .'

I come to a stunned halt. I was turning to look for a hardware store when I spotted something, just past the corner where I cut on to this stretch. I do a double take, but when I look again it's still there.

An artist's easel has been set in the middle of the road, straddling a white line. A medium-sized canvas rests on it. And just behind the easel stands a man, holding a painter's palette, gawping at me as if I'd come from another planet.

'Who the bloody hell are you?' I roar, striding towards him.

The man yelps and drops the palette. He turns and runs. I give immediate chase. He's faster than me, but I throw myself through the air, taking long jumps, and a few seconds later I overtake him and draw to a halt, blocking his way. The man screams and turns to run back the way he's come.

'Don't try it!' I shout. 'I don't need to breathe, so I can chase you all day and never drop my pace.'

The man shudders, glances around desperately for a place to hide or something to defend himself with. Finding nothing, he resigns himself, straightens and

turns to face me. He brushes dried flecks of paint from the sleeves of his coat and tries a shaky smile.

'My name is Timothy Jackson,' he squeaks, as posh as you like.

'What are you doing here?' I snap.

'Painting.' He nods at the easel and beams proudly, forgetting for a moment that he should be trembling with fear. 'I'm an artist.'

As I stare at him, lost for words, he mistakes my gaze for one of hunger and loses his confidence as quickly as he found it. With a gulp, his arms slump by his sides and he says in a low, miserable voice, 'Please don't eat me.'

ELEVEN

I circle the artist warily as he stands shivering and wincing. He's not very old, maybe early thirties. Medium height, a bit on the thin side, with a long face and dark circles round his eyes. He's wearing yellow trousers, a pink shirt and a tweed jacket. His clothes are dirty, ruined with paint, but look like they came from a top-notch shop. He has long, untidy brown hair, but is freshly shaven, not even a hint of stubble. He stinks of strong aftershave, like he bathes in the stuff.

I squint at the canvas on which he was working. It depicts the zombie hanging from the rope. The feet look too big, out of proportion to the rest of the body, but I suspect that's deliberate.

'Did you stick him up there?' I growl.

Timothy laughs nervously. 'Hardly. I found him here a few days ago and I've been coming back to paint him at different times of the day, to take advantage of the changing light.'

'He's suffering. Zombies can't endure the sun. He's burnt and going blind. You never thought about letting him down?'

Timothy blinks and scratches his head. 'To be honest, no, I didn't. It's not that I derive any pleasure from his pain – I feel sorry for these poor creatures – but if I'd set him free, he would have come after me and either gouged out my brain or turned me into a monster like him.'

I have to acknowledge that he's got a point.

'I'll let you off this time,' I sniff.

'If it's not impudent of me,' Timothy murmurs, eyes round and filled with curiosity, 'what on earth *are* you? I thought you were one of the undead when I first saw you, but then you spoke.'

'I'm a revitalised,' I tell him. 'A zombie who regained its thoughts.'

'That's possible?' he gasps.

'In some cases, yeah.'

'Does that mean there's a cure for the rest of them?'

I shrug. 'I don't think so.'

Although, now that I consider it, maybe it does. Perhaps a serum could be fashioned from my blood, one that could restore thought to all of the living dead. If I get rescued on Wednesday, I'll suggest that to the soldiers. I don't mind being a guinea pig, not if I can help bring peace to the world. Hell, maybe I'll end up being hailed as a hero. B Smith — saviour of mankind!

'Enough about me,' I grunt. 'What the hell is an artist doing in the middle of the road in a city overrun by zombies?'

'Capturing the apocalypse for the sake of posterity,' he beams. 'I've been doing this every day since London fell. Well, not for the first couple of weeks – it was too dangerous to venture out – but I've not missed a day since.'

'And you haven't been attacked in all that time?' I ask sceptically.

'Of course I have,' he chuckles. 'I've had to race for my life more times than I can count. There are tricks I've learnt to employ which help ward off interest – I don't come out if it's cloudy, I douse myself in strong cologne to mask my scent, I make as little noise as possible – but I get spotted and chased two or three times a day on average.'

I frown. 'How come you haven't been caught yet?'

'A healthy mix of skill and luck,' he says, then pauses. 'Do you have a name?'

'Of course. I'm B Smith.'

'And you're not going to eat me, are you, B?'

'Nah. You don't look that tasty,' I laugh.

'You won't snap suddenly, lose your mind and turn on me?' he presses.

'No.'

'You're a good zombie?'

I smile. 'I probably wouldn't go that far. But I'm not a killer.'

Timothy mulls that over, then nods to himself. 'In

that case, do you mind if we head back to my place? I don't like talking out here in the open. Sounds carry and zombies have a keen sense of hearing.'

'Where do you live?' I ask.

'Close by. I never venture too far from my studio. Come, we can chat on the way, and I'd love to show you my work. Are you interested in art at all?'

'Not really,' I mutter and his face falls. 'But if it's drawings of zombies and the city, I definitely want to have a look.'

Timothy's smile returns full force. 'Excellent!' Picking up his easel and palette, he heads down Bethnal Green Road, whistling jauntily, strutting like a peacock.

TWELVE

Timothy looks like a man without a care in the world, but I note the way he casts careful glances at the buildings on either side, keeping an eye out for zombies. He's not as reckless as he appears, although his very presence here proves that he's something of a daredevil.

He comes to the turn for Brick Lane and pauses. 'That's where we're headed,' he says, nodding at the street which used to contain London's most famous string of curry houses.

'We're not going for an Indian, are we?' I joke.

'Actually I've made use of the restaurants quite a lot,' he says seriously. 'I ran out of fresh food long ago, but the freezers are still working in many places. I can rustle you up an amazing chicken madras if you're hungry.'

'I'm a zombie,' I remind him. 'I only eat brains.'

He considers that. 'If you supplied the brains, I could probably do something with them. Mix them up in a korma perhaps.'

I burst out laughing. 'Anyone ever tell you you're a nutjob, Jackson?'

'Only Mother, Father, my teachers and friends.' He sighs. 'But they're all dead or eaten now, so I guess I had the last laugh. All joking aside, I love to cook, so if you want . . .'

'Thanks for the offer, but cooking might rob the brains of the nutrients I need. As far as I know, they have to be raw.'

That's nonsense, but it satisfies Timothy and spares me the job of telling him I'd rather eat straight from a corpse's head than risk one of his dishes.

Timothy starts walking again but doesn't turn into Brick Lane.

'I thought you said we were going that way.'

'We are,' he nods, 'but my studio is about halfway down. It's a narrow, dark street. I've boarded up most of the buildings close to mine, but zombies could be lurking somewhere along the way. I always go down the main road and cut in from there. You have to be careful if you want to survive around here.'

At the end of Bethnal Green Road we cut left on to Commercial Street.

'I adored the markets around here,' Timothy says. 'I often came over on a Sunday and spent the entire day milling around, sketching people, buying things I didn't need, sampling the many local varieties of fine cuisine.'

'Fine cuisine?' I snort. 'Bagels and curry?'

'Oh, there was much more than that,' Timothy insists. 'Pies and falafel and jellied eels for instance.'

'*You* ate jellied eels?'

'Why shouldn't I?' he blinks.

'I didn't have you pegged for the jellied eels sort.

My gran loved them, and my dad and his mates tucked into them sometimes, but I mean, come on, they were disgusting. Cold, bony bits of eel wrapped up in slimy jelly — you wouldn't feed that mess to a dog.'

'It was authentic East London,' Timothy protests.

'*I'm* authentic East London,' I tell him, 'and I wouldn't touch jellied eels with a bargepole.'

'Well, to each their own,' he says with a shrug.

We turn into a street lined with beautiful old houses. It feeds into Brick Lane and we come to a huge building, the old Truman Brewery. Timothy looks around to make sure no one – no *thing* – is watching, then fishes a key out of a pocket and hurries to a large, steel door. He opens it quickly and slips inside. I get an uneasy feeling – maybe this is a trap and I'm not the first revitalised he's lured back – but then I recall his yellow trousers and chuckle weakly. What sort of a bad guy would wear yellow pants?

Maybe it's just because I'm lonely, but I decide to trust my new-found friend. Putting my doubts behind

me, I step into the gloom of the building and try not
to show any signs of unease as Timothy gently swings
the oversized door shut and cuts us off from the outside
world.

THIRTEEN

THIRTEEN

Timothy throws a switch and lights flicker on all over the place. We're in a spacious room, the sort you might find in a warehouse. The windows have all been boarded over to keep in the light and keep out the zombies.

'Most of that was done before I came,' Timothy says, nodding at the planks nailed over the glass. 'There were five other people sheltering here then, including a security guard who was on duty when the zombies attacked.'

'What happened to them?' I ask.

'Two were captured by zombies over the following weeks. The others decided to make a break for freedom. The last I saw of them, they were heading for the river to search for a boat.'

'Why didn't you go with them?'

He looks at me as if I'm crazy. 'I told you, I'm a painter. I stayed behind to paint.'

Timothy leads me up a short set of stairs and into an even larger room. There are canvases everywhere, most of them blank, along with brushes, tins of paint, easels and all sorts of artistic bits and bobs.

'I loved the East End art scene,' Timothy says as we stride through the room. 'It felt natural that I come here once London fell. I originally meant to make camp in an ordinary house, but when I strolled up Brick Lane and realised this amazing space was occupied by humans and secure, I knew it was fate.'

We climb another set of stairs and come to a massive room. The windows have been boarded over here too, though some cracks have been left between the planks to let light through.

'Why the boards?' I ask. 'Surely you don't need them this high up.'

Timothy squints at me. 'Are you *sure* you're a zombie?'

I point to the hole in my chest.

'Good answer. But then why do you know so little about your kind?'

'I was locked up,' I tell him. 'I only broke free a few weeks ago and I've laid low most nights since then.'

'Well,' Timothy chuckles, 'the good news is that if you like climbing, you're in for a treat. Those bones sticking out of your fingers are extraordinarily durable. They'll dig into wood, brick, all sorts of substances. Determined zombies can scale the walls of old buildings like this.'

The room is crammed with canvases, but unlike those downstairs, these have been worked on. A few are hanging, but most stand on the floor, propped against the walls. In some places they're stacked twelve deep.

'When I first moved in, I thought I'd have all the space I'd ever need,' Timothy says as we slowly circle

the room, studying the paintings. 'But I didn't anticipate my muse calling to me so strongly. As you can see,
I've been prolific.'

The paintings are dark, ominous, creepy, full of zombies, corpses, deserted streets, spooky sunsets. Even
though I'm no art expert, they instantly give me a sense
of pain, suffering and loss. It's like stepping into a
gallery of Hell.

'Do you like them?' Timothy asks, chewing a nail,
trying to act as if he doesn't care about my answer.

'They're unbelievable,' I sigh and his face lights up.

'They *are* rather good, aren't they?' he chirps, picking up one of the canvases and beaming at it. It's a
painting of a young girl, her head cracked open, brains
spilling on to the pavement, face smeared with blood.
But the way he gazes at it, it could be a painting of a
bunch of flowers.

'To be honest, I was never the most skilled of artists,'
Timothy admits. 'But then the zombies rose up, everyone fled or was killed, I was left here virtually alone,
and something changed. It was like I woke up one
morning with a new gift.'

Timothy sets down the painting and moves on, looking at the canvases in much the same way that a zombie looks at human skulls.

'We're living in tragic, terrible times. I believe that I've been spared and given extra talent so that I can document the troubles. A higher force guides me, empowers me, protects me when I'm on the streets. I shouldn't have survived this long. The fact that I have . . .'

He falls silent and stares at the dark paintings. I can see that they mean everything to him.

'Do you believe in God?' Timothy asks me.

I shuffle uneasily. 'I dunno. I don't *not* believe, but I'm not sure.'

'I used to be uncertain too,' he says, then waves an arm around at the atrocities captured on the canvases. 'But who else could have done this to the world? Only the Almighty could have judged mankind and razed it to the ground in such brute, total fashion.

'I don't know why a loving God would do this to us,' he whispers. 'But if I keep on painting, and study that which I've created for long enough, I think I can find out.'

He steps up to one of the paintings, carefully lays his fingers on it and says softly, 'This isn't really the work of Timothy Jackson. These were fashioned by the hand of *God*.'

FOURTEEN

I think Timothy's a nutter, but I say nothing. If he wants to believe that God is working through him, I don't mind. As long as he doesn't try to convert me, he can believe whatever the hell he likes.

Timothy shows me round the rest of the building. His sleeping quarters are basic, just blankets and pillows laid on the floor in one corner of a small room. He has a larder full of canned goods and bottles of water, some wine and champagne too. Several small freezers full of bread, meat and other perishables.

He keeps a radio, but only turns it on once or

twice a week to catch up with any major breaking news.

'My greatest worry is that they'll bomb London,' he says. 'There was talk of it in the early days. Zombies are everywhere, but they're especially prevalent in the big cities. According to some reporters, the army chiefs discussed levelling the likes of London and New York. Wiser heads prevailed, but if the rumours are to be believed, the suggestion is still on the table. If they ever go ahead with that, I want to get my paintings out of here. I don't mind if I get blown to pieces, but if the world lost my work, it would be an absolute tragedy.'

As impressive as the paintings are, I don't think their loss could be classed as a global disaster. But I don't share that opinion with Timothy.

'Don't you get lonely?' I ask as we sit in the main room and Timothy tucks into a corned beef sandwich.

'Why should I?' he counters, nodding at the paintings. 'I have those for company. I work all the time when I'm awake and I only sleep for five, maybe six, hours at night. Although I must admit I've often felt exposed. It's dangerous for me out there on the streets, no one to help if I run into trouble. Maybe that's why you've been sent to me.'

'What do you mean?' I frown.

He smiles crookedly. 'I don't think we met by coincidence. It was fate. God wants you to become my bodyguard, to ensure my work can continue.'

As I stare at him, his smile widens. 'You can stay with me. I'll share all that I have, help you find brains, be company for you. We'll be a team, Jackson and Smith, doing the work of the Lord. Neither one of us need ever be alone again.'

That sounds both tempting and creepy at the same time.

'Did you have a partner before all this?' I ask, to change the subject.

He nods, his smile fading. 'Alan. He was a sculptor. He could create the most lifelike hands.'

'What happened to him?'

'He became one of *them*,' Timothy says emotionlessly. 'I went looking for him in his studio, but he'd already been infected. He chased me. Almost killed me.

I had to fight for my life. I managed to drive one of his chisels through his head.'

Timothy lays down his sandwich and stares ahead at nothing.

'That was when I created my first painting,' he says softly. 'I mixed Alan's blood with the paint, careful to don gloves before touching it. I painted him as he was, lying there, teeth bared in a death snarl, the handle of the chisel sticking out of his skull. I wept as I painted, knowing it was beautiful, yet hating it at the same time. Part of me – the part that loves, cherishes, cares – died that day. It was a part that needed to die. It would have got in the way of my work.'

He lapses into silence, his expression distant.

'Do you still have that painting?' I ask.

'No. I burnt it and scattered the ashes over Alan's corpse. It would have felt like theft if I'd taken it. That moment belonged to him. I didn't want to steal it.'

'But you've stolen all of these,' I murmur, waving at the canvases.

'Yes,' he sighs. 'I should feel guilty but I don't. I can't afford guilt or love or anything pure like that. To do my job, I have to be as passionless as the zombies I paint and run from.' He smiles fleetingly. 'That might be another reason why I've made it as far as I have. Maybe they realise, as they draw closer, that I'm not so different to them. In many ways I'm one of the walking dead as well . . .'

Later Timothy asks if he can sketch me before he hits the sack. I sit for him patiently while he stares at the hole in my chest and tries to bring it to life on a canvas. He shows it to me when he's done. My face is dimly painted with a mix of dark grey colours. All the focus is on the red and green mess around the hole where my boob should be. I hate the way I look in the drawing.

'You don't like it,' Timothy notes, disappointed.

'It's just . . . am I really that ugly?' I ask.

He shakes his head. 'You're not ugly at all. But you're a walking corpse. I have to show that, otherwise it won't ring true.'

'That's how I look to you?' I sniff. 'Pale, distant, vicious?'

'Not vicious,' Timothy corrects me. 'I would have said *hungry*. Not just for brains, but for your old life, a cure, the ability to be human again. You hunger for things you can no longer have, and that hunger brings you pain.'

I think about that hours later, while Timothy sleeps. I've stayed in the room of paintings, studying them silently, looking for familiar faces. I *am* in pain, all the time, and it's not just because I'm undead. I lost my parents and friends — whether they're dead, alive or somewhere between, I'll almost certainly never see them again. I threw an innocent boy to a pack of zombies. I killed humans when I turned. I failed to save Mark from the zom heads. I have blood on my hands. There's rot in my soul.

By rights, I should huddle up in a ball and howl, beg for pity, forgiveness, release. I should hurl myself off a tall building or find a gun and blow my brains out. In this cruel world, I can only experience more pain, ruin more lives, kill or infect. If Timothy stumbled when he was painting me, and I reached out to steady him, and one of my nails nicked his flesh ...

I stare at the monsters in the paintings. I'm no less monstrous than any of them. Maybe I'm worse, still being able to think. They have no choice in what they do, but I have. I could eliminate myself, make sure nobody ever suffered again at my twisted, wretched hands.

But I keep thinking about the possibility of revitalising the rest of the undead hordes. If my blood could be used to restore consciousness in other zombies, it might help bring order back to this crazy, lethal world.

In the morning, when Timothy awakes, I tell him I have to go.

'You're leaving?' He blinks sleepily. 'Did I say something to offend you?'

'No,' I smile. 'But I can't stay. There's going to be a rescue mission soon. I have to surrender, let the soldiers know I'm different, so their scientists can study me and maybe find a way to help other zombies think clearly.'

Timothy hums. 'The soldiers would, I imagine, be more inclined to execute you on sight.'

'Yeah, I know. But I have to try. You can come along too if you want.'

He smiles shyly. 'I can't leave. I belong here. I wish you luck, B, but your way isn't mine. If they reject you, please bear in mind that you will always be welcome in my studio.'

'Thanks.' I chuckle drily. 'I'd like to shake your hand, but . . .'

He chuckles too. 'One tiny scratch and I'd be history.'

'If I do get out,' I say hesitantly, 'is there anything you need, anything I can send back to you?'

He shakes his head. 'Just tell people about my work.' He gestures to the canvases. 'We'll all be here, the dead and I, waiting for the world to find us.'

'What if they don't want to find you?' I ask. 'People might not want to look at paintings of zombies, having seen so many of them in the flesh.'

'They will,' he insists. He walks over to the nearest painting, picks it up and gazes into the face of a monster. 'This is the truth, who we are and where we've come from. People are always drawn to the truth. It demands that we acknowledge it and learn.'

He closes his eyes and his face whitens.

'In the end, stripped bare of everything else, as everyone is eventually, all we're left with is the truth.'

I don't understand that, so I leave Timothy hugging his painting, eyes shut, lost to a world of madness or truth or whatever you want to call it.

FIFTEEN

I've loads of time on my hands, so I decide to do a bit of sightseeing as I'm making my way towards the centre of the city, and cut south towards the river.

I come to the Tower of London and stroll around the moat to the main entrance. Amazingly, I've never visited here before, not even on a school tour.

As I approach the gate, I spot a Beefeater standing in the shadows of a hut. He growls and steps forward, squinting in the light. Part of his throat has been bitten out and green moss grows round the hole like a wayward beard. I let him examine the gap in my chest.

Once he's had a good look, I start forward, but he stops me.

'Out of my way,' I snap, but when I try to wriggle past, he pushes me back. 'I'm one of you, idiot!' I shout, and shove him aside.

The Beefeater slams an elbow into the side of my head as I'm passing, catching me by surprise. I haven't seen any zombies fighting with one another. I didn't think I had anything to fear. Seems like I should have been more cautious.

As I stagger around, the inside of my skull ringing wildly, the Beefeater grabs me and hauls me to the ground. He pins me with his knees and makes a howling, gurgling sound before baring his teeth and leaning forward to chew through my skull.

I thought I'd be able to outsmart a zombie in a one-on-one struggle, but the Beefeater has me bang to rights. All I can do is stare at him with horror as he opens his mouth wide and presses his fangs to the cold flesh of my forehead.

For a few seconds the Beefeater holds that position. My sights are locked on the hole in his throat. If I could get a hand free, I could maybe rip the hole wide open. As I'm considering that, and wondering why the Beefeater has paused, he leans back and looks at me stiffly. To my astonishment he holds up a hand and makes a pinching gesture with his thumb and fingers. Then he cocks his head sideways, questioningly.

'You've got to be kidding,' I groan, realising what the issue is.

The Beefeater snarls and makes the gesture with his fingers again. He's a mindless, cannibalistic killer, but somewhere deep in that ruined brain of his, an old spark of instinct is driving him to do what he did every working day when he was alive.

'OK,' I wheeze. 'If you let me up, I'll play ball. I'm a good girl, I am.'

The Beefeater squints at me. I offer a shaky smile. He grunts and gets off, studying me suspiciously, as if he thinks I'm going to try and trick him.

Shaking my head with disbelief, I get to my feet and make for the ticket office which I passed on my way. The windows have been smashed in. I lean over the counter and grab a ticket from the nearest machine.

Returning to the gate, I hand the ticket to the jobs-worth of a zombie Beefeater. He takes it from me, nods gruffly and returns to his post, letting me through.

Unbe-bloody-lievable!

I go on a tour of the famous buildings, but most are packed with zombies – including a lot of overweight tourists who probably prefer their brains in batter and deep-fried – so I stick to the paths for the most part. I'm sorry I didn't come when it was operational. I couldn't care less about the Crown jewels, but I'd have loved to learn more about the prisoners who were held here and all the heads that were chopped off.

I recall the legend that if the ravens ever fled the Tower or died out, the city would fall. I always dis-missed that as a story most likely cooked up by a raven-handler who wanted to make sure he was never driven out of a job. But as I wander, I note glumly that there isn't a bird to be seen, apart from a few brittle bones, beaks and feathers.

Coincidence? Probably. But it gives me a mild dose of the creeps all the same. Did some scraggly, wild-eyed soothsayer predict this disaster all those centuries ago?

Was this plague of the living dead always destined to happen? Uneasy, I push on sooner than I'd meant to, waving goodbye to the Beefeater as I pass, no hard feelings. In an odd sort of way I respect him. He's stuck true to his principles, even in death. I don't mind that he roughed me up. In his position I like to think that I'd do the same.

I cross Tower Bridge. It hasn't escaped the turmoil unscathed. A plane came down in this area – I guess a zombie must have got onboard and caused chaos – and chunks of the wreckage are lying in the river where it crashed. On its way, it took out the two walkways at the top of the bridge, smashing straight through them. The towers that they were attached to weren't damaged. It's as if someone came along and snipped off the connecting tunnels with a giant pair of scissors.

Rubble from the walkways is strewn across the road and footpaths, so I have to zigzag my way across. I pause at the point where the two halves of the bridge meet. How cool would it be if I found the engine rooms and raised the drawbridge!

I grin as I imagine it, then shake my head regretfully.

Time might be on my side, but I don't have *that* much to play with. Besides, I'm not a child. I'm on a deadly serious mission. This is proper, grown-up business.

The strangely-shaped, glass-fronted mayor's building is gleaming in the sun, half-blinding me. I hurry on past and head for HMS *Belfast*, thinking I might go for a stroll around the deck. But as I approach, I spot humans onboard. They've barricaded the gangway and several are standing guard, heavy rifles hanging by their sides. As I stare at the living people, bewildered to find them here, one of them spots me, raises his gun and opens fire.

Yelping, I duck out of sight and wait for the bullets to stop. When they do, I take off my jacket and wave it at the people on the boat.

'Ahoy!' I roar, getting all nautical. 'My name's B Smith. I don't mean you any harm. I want to –'

The guy starts shooting again before I can finish. Bullets rip through my jacket and one almost blows a couple of my fingers off. Cursing, I drop the jacket, then yank it to safety. I don't know who the people on the boat are, but they clearly like their own company, and when someone's armed to the teeth and quick on the trigger, a wise girl gives them all the space in the world that they want.

I detour via Tooley Street. I remember Dad telling me that the London Dungeon used to be here before it moved. I always loved that ghoulish maze of torment and atrocity, but I don't think I'll ever bother with it again. This city of the dead boasts more than enough public horrors, like the hanging zombie on . . .

I stop and wince — the zombie who was dangling from the lamp post on Bethnal Green Road! I meant to free him when I left Timothy's place, but I forgot all about him. It's no biggie. In fact it seems ridiculous to worry about a single zombie in this city of monsters. But if I was in his position and someone had the power to set me free and didn't . . .

What if you free him and he ends up killing Timothy? part of me sulks as I turn to head back the way I came.

'That's life,' I shrug.

The zombie doesn't thank me when I cut him down, or show the least sign that he's grateful. Instead, having paused to sniff me in case I'm worth tucking into, he hurries away, seeking shelter, stumbling into anything in his path, unable to see clearly out of his almost totally white eyes.

Feeling more of a time-wasting fool than a good Samaritan, I retrace my steps and make it back to Tooley Street by early afternoon. Moving on, I slip past Southwark Bridge and cast a wary eye over the shell of the Globe. I never went to a show there – wild horses couldn't have dragged me – but I know all about this place. It's where they used to put on Shakespearean plays every summer.

As I consider the fact that nobody will ever stage a three- or four-hour version of *Hamlet* or *King Lear* here ever again, I break out into a smile and chuckle wickedly — the downfall of civilisation isn't *all* bad news!

SIXTEEN

I'm heading for the impressive-looking Tate Modern when I spot a small boat pulling up to the pier. I watch with astonishment as nine people pile out and march towards shore like tourists on a day trip.

But these aren't like any tourists I've ever seen. All nine – four men and five women – are dressed in blue robes. Their arms are bare. Each has a tiny blue symbol scrawled across their forehead. And they chant softly as they progress.

I hang back as the group ignores the art museum and heads on to the pedestrian bridge, which my dad used to call the Wobbly Bridge, since it wobbled so badly when it first opened that they had to close it for months to steady it up.

Something about these people unsettles me. They don't seem to be carrying any weapons, yet they're walking around openly. Hasn't anyone told them about the zombies?

I follow the group on to the bridge, wait until we're halfway across – St Paul's Cathedral towers ahead of us – then call out to them, 'Hey!'

They stop but don't turn. I edge closer, skin prickling, ready to dive over the side of the bridge if they produce guns from beneath their robes and open fire. But although the men and women glance at me as I slip past them, nobody reacts in any other way.

The woman at the head of the group studies me with a solemn expression as I stop before her. She's pretty, but has a pinched, stern face. Her hair is pure white – all the others have white hair too, which makes me think it's dye – so it's hard to judge her age.

'You are one of the restless dead,' the woman says, having noted the hole in my chest.

'Yeah.'

She cocks her head. 'I did not know that the undead could speak.'

'Most can't. I'm an exception.'

The woman nods, then spreads her arms wide. 'I am Sister Clare, of the Order of the Shnax. Have you come to attack us, foul creature of the lost?'

'No.'

'You have not come to slice open our skulls and feast on our brains?' she presses, pale blue eyes hard in the glaring sunlight.

'Not unless you want me to,' I joke.

'There!' the woman exclaims to those behind her. 'The blessings of the Shnax are with us, as I told you they would be.'

The people in the robes mutter appreciatively and bow their heads. Sister Clare basks in their adulation, then trains her gaze on me again.

'Are you a vile imp sent to guide us?' she asks haughtily.

'No,' I growl, resisting the urge to punch her on the nose. 'I saw you getting out of the boat and was curious. I wanted to warn you as well. It's dangerous here. The zombies –'

'We know all about them,' she interrupts. 'They are why we have come, to test our faith against theirs.'

'What are you talking about?' I frown. 'Zombies don't have any faith. They're brainless.'

'They are instruments of the dark forces of the universe,' she corrects me. 'By walking without fear among them, we will challenge those who work through their pitiful forms and reclaim this ground that they would steal from us. If you mean neither to help nor hinder us, then step aside or face the wrath of the Shnax.'

The woman waves a hand at me and glides past imperiously. The others follow, nodding and mumbling. A few smirk at me. One of the men touches the symbol on his forehead, then points at me as if to say, 'I've got my eye on you!'

I don't care much for Sister Clare or her sneering tone, but these weirdos have caught my attention. I can't resist following, to find out what they're up to. So, ignoring the fact that they don't care for my company, I trail after them as they cross the bridge and wander into the zombie-infested bowels of the city.

SEVENTEEN

The fearless members of the Order of the Shnax march to St Paul's and stop outside, chanting happily, beaming at one another. The sun is shining brightly and no zombies are on the streets. It's as if we have the city to ourselves.

Sister Clare leads the group on a full circuit of the cathedral, then heads east. I try to wring more information out of her as they proceed.

'You know you're all going to be killed.'

She raises an eyebrow. 'You might wish for our deaths, vulgar beast of the otherworld, but you will be disappointed. We have the power of the Shnax on our side. No harm will befall us.'

'What *are* the Shnax?' I press. 'Some sort of religious group?'

'We are of the true religion,' Sister Clare tells me and points a finger at the sky. 'The religion of the stars.'

'The stars . . .' the others echo dreamily, all pointing upwards.

'Celestial beings have always gazed down on us,' Sister Clare continues. 'Since the dawn of mankind they have encouraged us, rewarded us when we are deserving, punished us when we have sinned. They are the Shnax.'

'Aliens?' I laugh. 'Pull the other one!'

She smiles condescendingly. 'Like so many others, you can only mock. That is why you were turned into a pitiful mockery of the human form while we were spared. This world was disgusting, overcrowded with vain, petty humans. It needed clearing so that a fresh, clean civilisation could grow out of the ashes of the old.

'The Shnax would never have done this to us, since

they are creatures of love, but there are other forces at work in the universe, agents of destruction. The Shnax protected us from them in the past, but this time, for our own good, they let their foes wreak havoc. But they shielded the believers and kept us safe, so that we can guide the others who survived.'

I gawp at Sister Clare and the lunatics who follow her.

'You think that you know better than us,' Sister Clare smirks. 'I see it in your eyes, as lifeless as they are.'

'Come on,' I chuckle uneasily. 'You can't really believe that aliens did this or that they're guarding you.'

'If not the Shnax, then who?' she asks.

'The government ... scientists ... terrorists ... take your pick.'

She shakes her head. 'This apocalypse was not the work of humans. No mortal could have subjected the world to terrors on such a diabolic scale. Mankind has been culled. The weak have been cut down and set against the strong. It is the result of a godly hand, but there are no gods meddling in our affairs, only the Shnax.'

'Who told you about these aliens? Did you read about them in a magazine? See a show on TV?'

'They contacted me directly,' she sniffs. 'They spoke to me in dreams to begin with. Later I learnt to put myself into a trance and speak with them that way.'

'So you hear voices,' I murmur.

'Go ahead,' she snaps, her smile vanishing. 'Laugh at me. You won't be the first. But I told people this would happen. Nobody believed me until it was too late. Now that the worst has come to pass, people are starting to see that I was right. These are the first of my disciples, but they will not be the last. When we emerge from these haunted streets, alive and untouched, more will flock to our side. The survivors will see that I am the mouthpiece of the Shnax, and the world will finally offer us the respect which we are due.'

Sister Clare turns to the others and cries, 'Out of the darkness of the skies came the Shnax!'

'Out of the darkness!' they respond, heads bobbing, fingers twitching.

The fanatics carry on, wandering aimlessly. I think about abandoning them – I should be heading west, not wasting my time on these maniacs – but I'll feel bad if I leave them without at least trying to make them see sense.

'You can't really believe that aliens will save you from the zombies,' I challenge them.

'How else are we protected?' Sister Clare retorts smugly, waving a hand at the buildings around us. 'These are the homes of the damned, populated by the lost and vicious hordes, yet no monster comes out to attack us.'

'You've been lucky,' I argue. 'Sunlight hurts zombies. They rest up in the daytime. If you're still here when night falls . . .' I draw a finger across my throat.

Sister Clare scowls at me. 'You know nothing of these matters, child of the lost. Leave us be.'

'I know that you're mad,' I snap. 'And I know you don't truly believe what you're preaching. You'd put your lives fully on the line if you did.'

'What are you talking about?' Sister Clare asks, drawing to a halt.

'It's brave of you to come here,' I drawl, smiling tightly at the men and women in the robes. 'But you'd have come when it was dark if you wanted to prove beyond doubt that you were under heavenly protection. Or you'd go into one of these buildings, packed with the living dead, stand in the middle of them and chant away to your heart's content. But you don't because you know deep down that you'd be eaten alive.'

I flash my sharp teeth at them. Sister Clare's face reddens and she opens her mouth to have a go at me. But then one of the men says, 'The girl speaks the truth.'

Sister Clare's eyes fill with rage. 'You doubt me, Sean?' she shrieks.

'No,' the man called Sean says without lowering his gaze. 'I believe. But we must face our enemy. If the Shnax are looking down on us kindly, as I'm sure they are, we can walk through the ranks of the undead and the whole world will know that what we say is true. Otherwise people will sneer at us, as she has, and claim it was merely good fortune that we passed through these streets unharmed.'

Sister Clare licks her lips nervously. I catch a glimpse of uncertainty in her expression. Part of her knows this is madness.

'I can lead you back to your boat,' I say softly. 'You can return to wherever you were hiding before. You'll die if you go on.'

She stares at me for a long moment. Then she spits in my face. As I pull back, shocked, she faces her followers. 'The demon wants to lure us back to our boat and send us on our way. She is afraid of us, afraid of the Shnax.'

The other men and women start jeering and spitting at me. My temper flares and I flex my fingers, ready to rip them to pieces. I take a step forward, snarling. I think, if Sister Clare stepped away, I'd go for her. But she doesn't retreat. Instead she takes a step towards me, tilting her head back, offering her throat.

'Go ahead, servant of the darkness,' she hisses. 'Kill me if that is what your foul masters demand. I will die happily in the service of the Shnax.'

The others fall to their knees and offer their throats too. I shake my head and lower my hand, remembering Tyler Bayor, recalling my vow to be a better person.

Sister Clare tuts. Then her features soften. 'No, it is

wrong of me to blame you for what you have become. You were weak, as so many were, but it is not for us to condemn you. You are suffering enough.'

Her gaze settles on something behind me. She starts to smile again. 'But the imp is right about one thing, brothers and sisters. We *do* need to confront the forces of darkness directly, to prove beyond a shadow of a doubt that we are blessed. Let us face our destiny and show the world that ours is the one true way. Follow me!'

Sister Clare sets off at a jog. The others rise and hurry after her, chanting even faster than before, buzzing now, ready to follow their leader into the jaws of Hell if she demands it of them.

Turning to see where they're going, I realise she's leading them to a place even deadlier than the fabled gates of the underworld. We've come to the threshold of Liverpool Street Station. There are probably scores of zombies down there on the concourse, sheltering from the sun. Sister Clare is at the top of the steps which descend into that murky den of the dead.

'No!' I yell. 'Don't do it. I didn't mean to dare you.

I believe. You don't have to prove anything to me. Come back.'

But Sister Clare only flashes me a smile of twisted triumph. Then she heads down, followed by the others, into the zombie-friendly gloom.

EIGHTEEN

EIGHTEEN

I can't bear to let them go off by themselves, so I race after them, down the steps into the stomach of what was once commuter heaven.

It's not as dark down here as I thought. The station lets in quite a lot of light, so most of the zombies in residence have avoided the concourse. Still, there must be a hundred or more of the beasts who were resting in the shade around the main ring of the station. And every single one of them is now pushing forward, closing in on the nine robed, doomed humans.

Sister Clare acts as if she's unaware of the threat and

marches to the centre of the concourse. Her chant turns into a song and the others take it up, a dull tune about stars and aliens and how the chosen will be spared the wrath of the skies.

The deluded humans come to a halt in the middle of the station and form a circle, hands linked, feet planted firmly, singing joyously. The zombies push in closer . . . closer . . .

Then stop about a metre away.

I stare with disbelief at the white-haired men and women singing loudly, the zombies massed around them but not moving in for the kill, swaying softly as if held in place by the sound of the song. Or by something else?

It's crazy, but I find myself starting to wonder. As I slip through the ranks of the living dead, into the empty space around Sister Clare and her followers, I'm ready to believe. Why not? Their story makes as much sense as anything else in these bewildering times.

'You see?' Sister Clare whispers ecstatically. 'They're held in place by the power of the Shnax. They cannot raise a hand against those who are true.'

'This is incredible,' I croak.

'Yes,' Sister Clare says with justified satisfaction. Then she frees her hands and holds them over her head. 'We can break the circle now. Let us move among them. Show no fear. The Shnax will protect us as long as we continue to trust.'

Not all of the others look so sure about that, but they separate as ordered and edge forward.

The zombies don't budge.

'Part, sons and daughters of the darkness!' Sister Clare shrieks, swinging her right arm around like a scythe.

Not a single zombie gives ground.

One of the women loses her nerve and tries to push through, muttering sharply, 'Get out of my way!'

A zombie pulls her to the ground. He sinks his teeth into her exposed arm and tears loose a chunk of flesh. The woman screams.

'No!' Sister Clare shouts. 'Don't be afraid! Show no fear! We must be strong!'

But it's as if the scream acts as a starting pistol for the rest of the living dead. They surge forward, fingers extended, teeth bared, and throw themselves upon the stunned, defenceless children of the Shnax.

NINETEEN

The tortured death cries of the humans ring out loud. More zombies come running from within the Tube station attached to the railway concourse, not wanting to miss out on the feast.

I throw myself into the middle of the carnage and punch zombies aside, creating a narrow gap. 'This way!' I bellow.

I'm closest to Sister Clare, and she hasn't been attacked yet, so she's first past. She reels away from me and pushes through the divide, her face a mask of shock and fear. She starts to pause, but I shove her hard, careful not to pierce her flesh with my finger bones, aware that I'm as much of a threat as any revived.

'Run!' I roar at her, then try to pull some of the others free of the chaos.

Sean, the man who spoke up earlier when I was challenging Sister Clare, is the only one to get close to me. His eyes are bulging. His teeth are bared like the fangs of the monsters around us, but with terror, not hunger.

Then the finger bones of one of the zombies tear into Sean's chest, ripping through his robes, slicing into the flesh beneath. He stops and looks down at the wound. His fingers rise to touch it. All of the tension slips out of him. He smiles wearily at me, resigned to his fate. As I stare at him with horror, he spreads his arms and starts singing again. He carries on singing even when the zombies drag him down and chew through the bone of his skull, although towards the end it becomes more of a gurgling noise and the words are lost, along with the tune.

I don't stay to watch him die. As soon as I realise that the others are beyond help, I race after Sister Clare, determined to do all I can to save at least one of the nine, even though she probably deserves salvation the least of any of them.

Sister Clare was headed towards the stairs, but the zombies pouring through from the Tube station have blocked that route. As she hesitates, I call to her, 'I can see another exit at the far end. Follow me.'

We set off across the concourse. The way ahead is clear and I think we stand a chance. But then the zombies who couldn't get their hands on the other humans set their sights on Sister Clare and me — in the chaos, they won't be able to tell me apart from one of the living, so they'll tear into me too if they catch us.

A couple of seconds later it's clear we can't make it. Zombies stream into the path ahead of us, blocking the way. I draw to a halt and Sister Clare runs into my back. She tries to break past but I stop her.

'We're trapped.'

'No!' she screams. 'You've got to save me! Don't let me die!'

'I thought you were happy to die,' I grunt, but

bitterness won't do either of us any good. I look around desperately as the zombies close in. There's a row of shops to our right. The doors of most are wide open and the shops are totally indefensible. But a security grille has been pulled down over the front of one shop. It doesn't hang all the way to the ground, which means it isn't locked.

'There!' I yell, darting towards the shop. Sister Clare scurries along behind me. The zombies aren't much further back.

No time to mess about. I throw myself to the floor and push up the grille. As Sister Clare ducks and skids forward, I roll, slam down the grille and leap to my feet.

'I need something to hold this in place!' I shout, but Sister Clare is moaning, lying in a huddle on the floor, hands clamped over her ears. With a curse, I look around and spot a broom with a wooden handle. Grabbing it, I stick it through one of the slots in the grille, then jam it against the wall. It wouldn't hold back any thinking person for more than a few seconds, but the living dead aren't as sharp as they once were. Ignorant of the broom, they tug on the grille, trying to force it up, unable to figure out why it isn't moving.

I back away from the grille and sink to the floor beside Sister Clare. I stare at the zombies glumly. The broom won't hold for long. They'll push through in a minute or two and that will be the end of the human. Probably the end of me as well. The zombies are in a feeding frenzy. I'm guessing they won't pause to assess me, just dig straight into my skull and tear my brain out.

Sister Clare seems to realise she's still alive and lowers her hands, looking up with startled, fearful eyes. When she sees the zombies struggling with the grille, she smiles hopefully. 'You've stopped them.'

'Only for a while. If you want to pray to your aliens, you'd better be quick.'

'There must be a lock for the grille somewhere,' she pants, looking around frantically.

I snort. 'Even if we could find it and lock ourselves in, what's the point? They won't leave as long as they can hear your heartbeat and smell your brain. Better to die quickly and get it over with, rather than sit here and starve.'

'But there might be a way out the back.'

'We're underground,' I remind her. 'My finger bones are tough, but they can't burrow through walls.'

Sister Clare makes a low moaning noise, then grabs my arm and glares at me with some of her old determination. 'Then you have to convert me.'

'What?' I frown.

'Make me like you.' She points at the hole in my chest and the bones jutting out of my fingers. 'You're different. You can think and speak. If I end up like you, I can continue with my work.'

'*Continue?*' I splutter.

'We were weak,' she says. 'They attacked because they sensed our fear. If I was like you, I need not fear them. I could bring others here and they'd feed on my strength and certainty. We would triumph.'

'Are you even crazier than I thought?' I shout. 'You've already led eight people to their death. How many more do you want to sacrifice?'

'As many as the Shnax demand,' she snaps. 'They

wish to save us, but they can only do that if we're strong. Please, help me, don't let me be eaten, give me the power to continue with my mission.'

'Even if I wanted to, I couldn't. I don't know how –'

'Please!' she screams, not wanting to hear the truth, clasping her hands over her ears again.

I stare at the deranged woman, lost for words. Then a cruel part of me whispers, *Why not? She's doomed anyway. She lured her followers to their death and made fools of them. It's only fitting that you should do the same to her.*

'All right,' I tell her, pulling her hands away from her ears. 'We'll do it if you're sure. Are you?'

'Yes,' she gasps.

'Then on your own head be it,' I snarl, and pull her in close, as if to kiss her. But instead I bite into her lower lip, drawing blood and infecting her with my undead germs.

'Vile girl!' Sister Clare snaps, pushing me away and wiping blood from her lip. 'How dare you press your mouth to mine! I should ...'

She raises a hand to slap me. Then she realises what

I've done and backs away, whimpering softly, staring at the blood on her fingers.

'You bit me,' she whispers.

'Yeah,' I say, feeling rotten now that the moment has passed.

'Will I retain my senses?' she cries. 'Will I become like you, not like *them*?' She points at the zombies pulling at the grille.

'Of course,' I lie, not knowing if it's true or not, wanting to give her some comfort in her final moments.

'Wonderful,' she sighs, leaning against the wall, waiting for the change, probably privately plotting her undead takeover of the world.

Sister Clare shudders. She bends over, gasps, collapses, then screams as her body starts to shut down. I turn away, not wanting to see her teeth lengthen, the bones break through her fingertips, the light fade from her eyes.

The handle of the broom snaps. The grille clatters upwards. Zombies spill into the shop and swarm around us.

But they don't attack, because they can see the

human turning. That makes them pause and they sniff me rather than strike. When they realise I'm one of them, they leave us be and return to the concourse, disappointed and hungry.

After about a minute, I look around guiltily. Sister Clare is staring at me numbly, no hint of life in her expression, green moss already sprouting from the bite mark on her lip.

'Sorry,' I murmur. 'But you did ask for it.'

Making a sighing sound, I blow a regretful kiss to the shadowy remains of Sister Clare, then push through the undead crowd outside the shop, patiently easing my way clear of the crush, past the bodies of the humans who were killed, up the stairs and back into the light of a world which seems even more lost and disturbing than it did an hour or two before.

TWENTY

I make my way west, then hole up in an abandoned coffee shop on Fleet Street when night falls. Every time I think about Sister Clare and her pack of nutjobs – and I think about them lots over the course of the night – I wince sadly. What a waste of life.

I feel guilty too, for biting Sister Clare, knowing it was almost certain that she wouldn't end up like me, that she'd become just another mindless revived.

'The zombies would have killed me if I hadn't done it,' I whisper.

'*So?*' I snort.

'I needed to get out,' I argue, 'to hand myself over to the soldiers, so that they can use my blood to maybe find a way to defeat the zombies.'

'*Yeah,*' I retort cynically. '*If they don't shoot me first.*'

'I've got to think positively.'

'*In this world?*' I sneer. '*Get real!*'

The night passes slowly. I hear the dead milling around outside, searching for prey, but no screams or gunfire. If any of the living are heading towards the centre to be rescued, they're lying low like me. That's not surprising. Only the cunning will have lasted this long. Smart operators like that are hardly going to give themselves away cheaply this close to escape.

As the sun rises and the zombies return to the shadows, I move out and push on, hitting the Strand. Finding a radio in a shop, I tune into the news channel and wait. It's not long before an excited presenter says that the rescue is scheduled for midday in Trafalgar Square. He tells anyone who is listening to make sure they're present at twelve on the dot, but not to show themselves in the square before that, in case they attract unwanted attention.

I head down the Strand, taking my time. I swing right and check out Covent Garden, once a throng of tourists, shoppers and street performers. I'm half-hoping to find some zombie jugglers, maybe throwing limbs around instead of skittles or juggling balls, but the place is as dead as any other part of London.

I pick up new clothes for myself in one of the fashionable designer shops, so that I look fresh and clean. I think about tearing a hole in my jumper and T-shirt, to expose the empty cavity, but decide to leave it as it is for the moment, so that I can get close to the soldiers before they realise I'm a zombie.

I file down my teeth and the bones sticking out of my fingers and toes. The bones are harder to disguise than the hole in my chest. I pull on a pair of shoes which are three sizes too big for me, and gloves that are more suited to a giant. The shoes are uncomfortable, and the gloves won't hide the shape of the bones up close, but they should get me near and give me a chance to make my case.

I also pick up a pair of watches which would have cost almost as much as our flat in the old days. They're accurate to the smallest fraction of a second, resistant to shock, waterproof, and they automatically adjust for summer or winter time. I attach one to either wrist, so that I can be absolutely sure of the time. I don't want to miss my shot at rescue because of a dodgy watch!

I get to Trafalgar Square five minutes before midday. I'm not the first to arrive. Seven people are already present, three men, a woman with a baby, a girl of eight or nine and a boy a bit younger than me. They're huddled together in the middle of the square, between the two fountains, ignoring the warning not to arrive earlier than twelve. I was expecting warriors, tough men in leathers, carrying guns. But this lot look like any group of tourists that you would have seen here a year ago.

'Are you one of us?' the woman with the baby shouts when she spots me striding towards them.

'That depends — who are you?' I shout back.

They relax at the sound of my voice. They obviously don't know about talking zombies or they wouldn't be so trusting.

Others come out of the shadows as I draw closer to

the group in the centre. Two from the direction of the Mall, one from behind the Fourth Plinth, three more – not together, but separately – from Whitehall. They approach cautiously, checking out the buildings as they creep along, keeping to the middle of the road.

I was worried that the people at the heart of the square might grow suspicious if I kept my distance, but to my relief the other newcomers hang back too, not willing to associate too closely with strangers, ready to make a break for freedom if anything goes wrong.

There's no cheerful banter. Apart from the seven in the middle, who mutter among themselves, nobody speaks. Everyone looks wary, studying the others suspiciously, scanning the buildings around the square for signs of life — or, to be more accurate, *un*life.

At twelve o'clock exactly, four helicopters buzz into view overhead. They're military vehicles, armed with missiles and machine guns.

The helicopters do a few circuits over the square, checking to make sure that everyone beneath them is human. Some of the people cheer and wave. I don't. I'm not sure if the soldiers will view me as a friend or an enemy, so I don't want to draw their scrutiny until I have to.

Satisfied with what they see, three of the helicopters set down on the terrace at the top of the steps, between the square and the National Gallery. The fourth remains airborne, hovering ominously, the pilot keeping watch over the others, ready to support them from the air if necessary.

Four soldiers slide out of each helicopter. The pilots remain in place, engines running, rotors whirring. The noise is deafening, especially with my advanced sense of hearing. I grit my teeth and try not to show any signs of distress, not wanting to appear different to the other survivors.

The twelve soldiers advance to the top of the steps. Everyone in the square has started moving towards them. A couple of people are running. But before anyone can set foot on the stairs, two of the soldiers open fire with their rifles and spray the steps with bullets.

As we come to a shocked halt, one of the soldiers moves forward and addresses us through a megaphone.

'No need to panic, people,' he barks. 'We've done this before, so we know what we're doing. We're going to get all of you out of here, but there are rules you have to obey. We've put them in place for your safety as well as ours, to ensure no infected specimens sneak through.'

'We're not infected!' one of the men yells. 'You can see that by looking at us!'

'Looks can be deceptive,' the soldier replies. 'We don't take risks. I'm sure you can appreciate our position, and the fact that the more cautiously we proceed, the safer you'll all be. We want to get you out of here as swiftly as possible, so listen up and do what you're told.'

'This is crazy!' the man roars, starting forward indignantly. 'Zombies could be closing in on us while you're wasting time. Let us through.'

'If you take one more step, sir, you *will* be executed,' the soldier snaps. As the man hesitates, he continues. 'We'll do all that we can to help you, but if we sense a threat, we'll eliminate it, no questions asked. You *do not* want to push us.'

The man gulps, raises his hands and takes three big steps back.

'OK,' the soldier says. 'Here's how it works. First you're going to undress. No need to be shy, we've seen it all before. Once you're naked, you'll approach one by one as we summon you, leaving your clothes behind. We'll check you quickly, make sure you're clean, then you can collect your gear and board the helicopters. When we've loaded everyone up, we're out of here.'

The other people grumble but begin stripping off, wanting to escape this city of the dead more than they want to protect their modesty.

I don't take off anything. Instead I wave my hands over my head and call to the soldier. 'Sir!'

The soldier smirks at me. 'I told you there was no need to be shy. Don't worry, girl, nobody's going to take photos of you.'

'That doesn't bother me. But I'm . . . I'm not like the rest of them.'

His smile disappears in an instant. He takes a closer look at me, my hat, the sunglasses, the gloves and shoes.

'Take off your gloves,' the soldier growls. Something

in his voice alerts the others and everybody pauses and stares at me. The soldiers adjust their guns. They're all pointing in my direction now.

'I don't want to cause any trouble,' I cry, not moving in case I set off a trigger-happy marksman.

'Remove your gloves!' the soldier with the megaphone roars.

'I will,' I moan. 'I'm doing it now.' I lower my hands and start to peel off the gloves, slow as I can. 'But you're going to see bones. And when I take off my clothes, you'll see –'

'She's infected!' a soldier shouts, and some of the people in the square start to scream.

'No!' I shriek, raising my hands again and waving them over my head. 'I want to help. I came here to offer my services.'

'Screw that,' the soldier with the megaphone snaps. 'I told you we don't take chances. Fire!'

Before I can say anything else, every soldier in the square starts shooting, and the nightmarish bellow of their guns drowns out even the ear-shattering thunder of the helicopter blades.

TWENTY
-ONE

The soldiers' reaction hasn't come as a complete shock.
I hoped this wouldn't happen but I half-expected it. So
when I was edging forward a few minutes ago, I carefully
positioned myself by one of the fountains, just in case.

As the soldiers rain down hell on me, I hurl myself
to my right, into the dried-out fountain. The bullets
pound the base. Stone chips and splinters fly in all
directions and the piercing whine makes me gasp with
pain. But I'm safe for the moment. They can't hit me
from where they are, not unless I do something stupid
like stick my head up.

The soldiers stop firing and the one with the megaphone shouts at the rest of the people. 'This is why we have rules! Get your damn clothes off as quick as you can or we'll shoot the lot of you!'

'We didn't know she was one of them!' a woman screams. 'We'd never seen her before. She spoke to us. How can she speak if she's dead?'

'The dead have all sorts of tricks up their sleeves,' the soldier says. 'Now show us your flesh, and hurry, before the noise brings scores of curious zombies down upon us.'

While the people are undressing, I roar at the soldiers, 'There's no need to do this. I want to help. If you don't want my help, fine, I'll leave you be. But I'm different to the other zombies. Maybe you can take some of my blood and –'

'I don't want to hear it!' the soldier yells. 'Just shut up and play dead, you damn zombie bitch!'

'Up yours, numbnuts!' I retort angrily.

'Right, that's enough,' he snarls, then barks a command into his radio.

Overhead, the airborne helicopter buzzes forward.

I've seen enough war movies to know what's coming next. With a yelp, I throw myself out of the fountain. My right shoe flew from my foot when I leapt in, and now my left drops away too. But the shoes are the least of my worries. Because as I scramble clear, the pilot hits a button and launches a missile.

The fountain explodes behind me and I'm tossed clear across the square by the force of the explosion. I slam into a lamp post and slump to the ground. My ears are ringing. The hat and glasses have been blown from my head. I'm half-blind and all the way shaken.

Sitting up in a wounded daze, I catch a blurred glimpse of the helicopter gliding in for the kill. I've nowhere to hide now and no strength to push myself towards safety even if I did. Spitting out thick, congealed blood, I sneer at the pilot – just a vague, ghostly figure from here – and give him the finger, the only missile in my own personal arsenal.

There's another explosion. I can't shut my eyes against it, so I cover them with a scratched, bloodied hand instead. Flames lick across the sky and I feel like I'm being sunburnt in the space of a few sizzling seconds. There's a roaring, maniacal sound, as if two huge sheets of welded-together metal are being wrenched apart. Then the dull thudding noises of an impossibly heavy rainfall.

None of this makes sense. The second explosion should have been the end of me. B Smith blown to bits — goodbye, cruel world. But I'm still alive and there's a gap in the sky where the helicopter should be. What the hell?

Lowering my hand, I peer through a dust cloud which has risen in front of me like a shroud. As it starts to clear, I see the wreckage of the helicopter scattered across the ground, mixed in with the remains of the fountain. Some bones jut out of the mess, all that's left of the pilot and any soldiers who were with him.

I gawp at the bewildering scene, then look up at the steps. And that's when everything clicks into sudden, sickening focus.

A second armed force has spilled out of the National Gallery. Dozens of people, more appearing by the second, racing down the steps at the side of the pillared entrance, or leaping over the railing to land directly on the terrace. One of them has a bazooka. Smoke is spiralling from its muzzle.

The troops spewing out of the art museum are neither human nor zombies. Most are wearing jeans and hoodies. Their skin is disfigured, purple in places, peeling away from the bone in others, full of ugly, pus-filled wounds and sores. They have straggly grey hair and pale yellow eyes. I can't see from here, but I know that inside their mouths their few remaining teeth are black and stained, their tongues scabby and shrivelled, and if they spoke, the words would come out snarled and gurgled.

These are the mutants I spotted in the Imperial War Museum shortly before the zombie uprising, the same monstrous creatures who stormed the underground complex. I know no more about them now than I did then, except for two things. One — they cause chaos whenever they appear. Two — they're led by a foul being even weirder than they are.

As if on cue, as the mutants tear into the startled soldiers, I spot him emerging behind them, colourful as a peacock set against the grey backdrop of the National

Gallery. He stands between two pillars, arms spread wide, grinning insanely, the pink, v-shaped gouges carved into the flesh between his eyes and lips visible even from here, through the dust and with my poor eyes.

I can't see the badge that he wears on his chest, the one with his name on it. But I know that if I could, it would read, as it did when I first met him underground on that night of spiders and death, *Mr Dowling*.

Send in the clown!

TWENTY -TWO

The mutants swarm round the soldiers and helicopters. They're soon joined by a pack of zombies, who follow them out of the National Gallery, shaded from the sun by long, *Matrix*-style leather jackets, huge straw hats and sunglasses. I'm sure the jackets, hats and glasses were chosen for them by Mr Dowling.

Two of the helicopters are overrun before their pilots can react. The third manages to clear the ground, but then the mutant with the bazooka reloads, takes aim and fires. It comes crashing back to earth, taking out the bottom section of a building where a bookshop once stood.

The soldiers fight doggedly, first with their guns, then with knives and their hands. But there are too many mutants and zombies. Within a minute the last of the human troops has been cut down and Trafalgar Square belongs to Mr Dowling and his warped warriors.

A few of the people who came to be rescued have made a break for freedom. They race from the square, hounded by a handful of whooping mutants and hungry zombies. The others are huddled together in the centre, surrounded, trapped, alive for the moment but undoubtedly doomed.

Some of the zombies focus on the humans and move in for the kill, but stop when a mutant blows a whistle. I've seen this before — Mr Dowling's henchmen have the power to command the living dead.

The mutants jeer at the weeping, shrieking humans and stab playfully at them with knives and spears, not interested in wounding them, just in winding them up. I want to try and help, cause a disturbance, break through their ranks and create a gap for the others to escape through. But I can only sit, dazed, ears ringing, legs useless, and watch.

Mr Dowling trots down the steps of the National Gallery at last, doing a little dance as he descends. The mutants applaud wildly and screech at the humans to clap too.

As the clown nimbly waltzes down the steps from the terrace to the square, I get a clearer look at him. The flesh of a severed face hangs from each shoulder of his jacket. Lengths of human guts are wrapped round his arms, and severed ears are pinned to his trouser legs. A baby's skull sticks out of the end of each of his ridiculously large red shoes. His hair is all different sorts of colours and lengths, torn from the heads of others in clumps and stapled into place. The flesh around his eyes has been cut away and filled in with soot. Two v-shaped channels run from just under either eye, down to his upper lip, and the bone beneath has been painted pink. A human eye has been stuck to the end of his nose and little red stars are dotted around it.

The trapped humans stop screaming as the clown

approaches and the mutants pull back to let him through. Like me, these people have seen a lot since the world went to hell, but nothing like this. Mr Dowling belongs to another dimension entirely, one even crazier and more twisted than this undead hellhole.

To conclude his dance, Mr Dowling leaps into the air and pirouettes, then drops to one knee and spreads his arms wide. The mutants howl their appreciation and stamp their feet raucously. One of them holds up a sheet of paper with a large 10 scrawled across it in red.

Mr Dowling bows his head and accepts the acclaim with false humility. Then he hops back to both feet and prowls round the humans, grinning at them like a piranha, his eyes twitching insanely, skin wriggling as if insects are burrowing about beneath the flesh.

One of the mutants steps up next to the clown and blows his whistle sharply, waving an arm for silence. I could be wrong, but I think it's the one who tried to kidnap a baby in the Imperial War Museum on the day when I first learnt that this wasn't just a world of normal humans.

When all of the mutants are still, the one with the

whistle addresses the sobbing people at the heart of the crush in a choked, gurgly voice.

'Ladies, gentlemen and children — it's show time! Welcome to the weird, wild, wonderful world of Mr Dowling and his amazing cohorts. Thrill to the sight of the living dead and their masters. Coo as we rip you from head to toe. Cheer as we make intricate designs out of your gooey innards. Worship as we take you to Hell and beyond.'

The mutants cheer again, but the humans only stare in bewilderment. Most of them are weeping openly. 'Please!' one of the men begs. 'Spare us! We're not . . . we won't . . . anything you ask of us . . .'

'Hush,' the mutant frowns. 'Mr Dowling did not come here to entertain futile pleas. He came to party!'

'*Party!*' the mutants holler, shaking their fists and weapons over their heads.

When they're silent again, Mr Dowling points a long, bony finger at the woman with the baby and makes a shrill squeaking noise. The mutant next to him listens carefully, then crooks a finger at the woman and beckons her forward.

'No!' a man next to her shouts. 'Take me, not the baby!'

'As you wish,' the mutant shrugs. He blows his whistle and a pair of zombies lurch into action, grab the man and drag him to the ground. His screams ring loud around the square, but not for long.

'Now,' the mutant says pleasantly, crooking his finger at the woman again.

She stumbles forward, shaking her head, crying, clutching the baby to her chest. 'Please,' she whispers. 'Please. Please. Please.'

The mutant makes a soothing, tutting noise, then prises the baby from her and hands it to Mr Dowling. The clown takes the child with surprising gentleness and rocks it in his arms. The baby gurgles happily, unaware of the danger it's in. Mr Dowling makes another sharp, questioning noise.

'Is it a boy or a girl?' the mutant asks politely.

'A guh-guh-guh-girl,' the woman gasps, eyes on her child, fingers clasped in silent prayer, rooted to the spot, helpless and terrified.

The clown nods slowly and squeals again.

'Mr Dowling says that he's glad,' the mutant translates. 'He's not in a boyish mood today. If it had been a boy, he would have dashed its head open and fed its brain to our zombies. But since it's a girl, he's inclined to be merciful.'

'He ... he's not going to hurt her?' the woman croaks, tearing her eyes away from the baby and looking to the mutant with the slightest glimmer of hope.

'That depends on the choice you make,' the mutant says.

'*Choose* ...' the other mutants murmur. The word sounds obscene on their scabby, twisted tongues.

'I don't understand,' the woman frowns.

'It's very simple,' the mutant grins. 'The ever-generous Mr Dowling is giving you a choice. You can choose to spare your baby or your colleagues.' He nods at the other humans in the square.

'You mean ...' She gulps, eyes widening.

'You got it, sweet thing,' the mutant chuckles obscenely. 'We butcher the baby or we kill everybody else. Your call. Now — choose.'

'*Choose . . .*' the others repeat again, their pale yellow eyes alive with repulsive yearning.

As the woman struggles with her choice, someone squats next to me and says, 'As distasteful as this is, it should be intriguing. Mr Dowling always puts on a memorable show.'

I look around in a daze. The man is tall and thin, but with a pot belly. He's wearing a striped suit with a pink shirt. He has white hair and pale skin, long fingers and unbelievably large eyes, twice the size of any normal person's, almost fully white, but with a tiny dark pupil burning fiercely at the centre of each.

'*Owl Man*,' I moan.

TWENTY -THREE

'You remember me,' the man with the owl-like eyes beams. 'How sweet.' He winks, then blows me a mocking kiss.

'This can't be real,' I mutter. 'I must be dreaming.'

'Don't be silly,' Owl Man tuts. 'You cannot sleep, so it follows that you cannot dream. Therefore this must be real.'

'It could be a hallucination.'

'Possibly,' he concedes. 'But it isn't. Now tell me, are you hurt? Can I help you?'

He reaches out a hand. I push myself away from his

creepy-looking fingers and wipe dirt and blood from my forehead. 'How are you here?' I ask. 'The last time I saw you was in my bedroom.'

'There's no telling who you might run into these days,' he smiles. 'The world was always a small place, but now it's positively box-like. So few of us left with our senses intact. Our paths cannot fail to cross.'

Owl Man stands and stretches. I frown as I study him.

'What are you? I can hear your heartbeat, so you're not a zombie. But you're not a mutant either, are you?'

'Certainly not,' he says, sniffing as if offended. 'I am ...' He pauses, thinks for a moment, then shrugs. 'I am, as you so poetically put it, *Owl Man.* That is all you need to know about me for now.'

My mind is whirring. There are so many questions I want to put to him, about the mutants, Mr Dowling, why certain zombies revitalise. I've a feeling that if anyone can answer those questions, it's him.

But before I can ask Owl Man anything, the mutant with the whistle shouts at the woman faced with the impossible choice. 'Time's up. Choose or we slaughter them all, baby, adults, the lot.'

Owl Man grimaces. 'Kinslow is a nasty piece of work, but he keeps things interesting, and that's what Mr Dowling demands of his followers.'

I get the sense that Owl Man doesn't approve of what's going on. But he doesn't try to stop it, just observes the sick show with a neutral expression.

'Hurry!' the mutant called Kinslow croaks. 'Choose now or . . .' He produces a knife and passes it to Mr Dowling. The clown laughs as he takes it, then slides the blade up beneath the baby's chin.

'*Them!*' the woman howls, falling to the ground with horror. 'Take them! Spare my child!'

The other people scream with fear and outrage, but their cries are cut short when Kinslow blows his whistle again, three long toots. At his command the living dead surge forward and tuck into the hapless humans, survivors no longer, just zombie fodder now.

'This is awful,' I groan, turning my gaze away.

'Yes,' Owl Man says morosely. 'But it's about to get even worse. Look.'

Mr Dowling hasn't handed back the baby. As the zombies finish off the last of the humans and tuck into fresh, warm brains, the clown strides among them, still clasping the infant. Kinslow and the woman trail after him, the mutant snickering, the woman distraught.

'My girl,' she whimpers, reaching for the baby.

'In a minute,' Kinslow snaps, pulling her back. 'You don't want to disturb Mr Dowling when he's preoccupied. You wouldn't like him if he lost his temper.'

The clown comes to a halt over a thin, male zombie who is digging into the open head of the boy who wasn't much younger than me. He watches the zombie for a while, then sticks his left index finger into a hole in the man's throat, where he was bitten when still alive. His finger comes out wet and red. With a soft, choking noise, he puts the finger into the baby's mouth and the little girl's lips close on it trustingly.

'*No!*' the girl's mother screams, sensing the threat too late to prevent it. She tries to throw herself at the clown, but Kinslow kicks her legs out from beneath her and she collapses.

'No! No! No!' she screeches, covering her ears with

her hands as the baby's brittle bones extend and snap through the skin of her fingers and toes. 'You told me you'd spare her! You promised!'

'We did spare her,' Kinslow says, taking the zombie baby from Mr Dowling and holding her out to the woman who was once her mother. 'She still lives, in a fashion. She's as wriggly and alert as ever. Just a little less . . . *breathy*. Now take her. She's yours to do with as you wish.'

Kinslow presses the baby into her mother's arms. Her tiny sharp teeth, newly sprouted, snap together as she stares at the woman whose brain smells so good and tempting, even to one as young as this.

The woman gazes down on her ruined child for a full minute in horrified silence, the clown and Kinslow waiting to see what she'll do next, everybody watching with wretched fascination except for the feasting zombies. Then, like a person sleepwalking, she undoes the buttons on her shirt and frees a breast. She presses her daughter to it and lets the undead baby bite and feed, murmuring softly to her, stroking her hair, vowing to care for her even in death.

'A touching scene,' Owl Man murmurs.

'Bastard,' I snarl at him.

'There's no point blaming me,' he says. 'I wasn't responsible.'

'You didn't do anything to stop it though, did you?' I challenge him.

'That's not my role,' he says. 'We all have a role to play in life, and unlike many unfortunate souls, I am all too aware of what the universe demands of me. I simply follow the path that destiny demands, as we all must.'

'Even if it means letting babies be sacrificed?' I sneer.

'Yes,' Owl Man whispers and a sad look crosses his oversized eyes. 'You may find this hard to believe, but I have done even worse than that in my time. I fear that you might too, over the course of the grim days and nights to come.'

'What are you talking about?' I snap.

'Remember when you could dream? Remember the babies on the plane?'

I shiver at the memory. Owl Man also asked me about my dreams the last time we met. 'What about the bloody nightmares?' I growl.

'They marked you, Becky,' he says. 'I was sure you would survive and regain your senses, just as I was certain we would meet again. You are a creature of the darkness, the same as myself and Mr Dowling. Like us, I fear that you too will end up destined to play a cruel, vicious part in the shaping of the future. Some of us cannot escape the damnable reach of fate.'

Before I can ask Owl Man what that means, he stands and calls to Kinslow and Mr Dowling. 'I have someone here I think you might be interested in.'

The clown bounds across, Kinslow racing to keep up. Mr Dowling stops in front of me and beams as if to welcome an old friend.

'You made it out,' Kinslow grunts, pulling up beside his master. 'Mr Dowling said that you would. You caught his eye underground. He told me you were the cream of the crop.'

'See, Becky?' Owl Man mutters. '*Marked.*'

Kinslow glares at the tall man with the owlish eyes, but says nothing.

Mr Dowling bends over until his face is in front of mine. The last time he did that, he spat a shower of spiders over me. But today I can't see anything in his mouth, only a long, black tongue.

The clown smells worse than an open sewer. My nose wrinkles and I try to turn my face away, but he grabs my chin and forces me to maintain eye contact. As he stares into my soul with his beady, twitching eyes, he squeals a few times, softly.

'He wants to know if you're ready to come with us,' Kinslow says. 'He knows that you disapprove of many of the things we do. But he's willing to teach you, spend time with you, show you the way forward, share his power with you.'

'He's out of his tiny mind if he thinks I'll ever have anything to do with you lot,' I jeer. 'You're freaks, every last damn one of you. I wouldn't spit on you if you were on fire, even if I *could* spit.'

The clown tilts his head sideways and frowns.

'You should kill her for saying a thing like that,' Kinslow growls.

'Mr Dowling decides who to kill and who to spare,' Owl Man thunders, his smooth voice dropping several octaves in the space of a heartbeat, his eyes flaring.

'Don't ever forget that or speak out of turn again. He makes the calls, not you.'

'Of course,' Kinslow says quickly, fear mixed in with his apology. 'I meant no disrespect. I was merely –'

'Shut up if you want to live,' Owl Man says lazily, then looks to the clown. 'I told you she would not come with us. Do you want to crack her skull open or let her go?'

The clown stares at me for a few seconds. Then he makes a chuckling, wheezy sound, turns and sets off across the square, Kinslow hurrying to keep up with him.

Owl Man winks at me, all smiles again. 'He said we'll probably end up killing you, but not today. He's in a good mood after the game with the baby. Go with his blessing, but bear this in mind — no matter where you go, no matter what you do, he knows you're out there and he can find you any time he likes. You haven't seen the last of Mr Dowling, Becky, not by a long shot.'

Owl Man peels away and follows the mutants and their master. I watch numbly as the clown gathers his posse and leads them from the square. Someone starts to sing an old ballad about murder and revenge, and by the time they pass from sight, they've all joined in, one big, happy party, heading off in search of fresh pickings, leaving me to fester in the square, surrounded by the wreckage of the helicopters and the cooling bodies of the dead.

TWENTY -FOUR

I remain in Trafalgar Square overnight, barely moving, staring at nothing, wishing somebody would come along and free me from this unholy hell of an existence. Zombies trail through the square over the course of the night, scraping dry the skulls of the corpses, ridding them of every last scrap of brain. Some come sniffing to make sure I'm not edible too. I ignore them and focus on the empty feeling inside, remembering the baby, the mutants, Owl Man, the clown, the blood-shed.

In the morning, as the sun rises and the carnage is

revealed in all its gory glory once again, I push myself to my feet, pick up my trusty Australian hat which is lying nearby, dusty but undented, and turn my back on the grisly scene. I'm in a universe of pain, and limp badly as I shuffle away, but my wounds aren't fatal. I'll survive, worse luck.

In a numb daze, I start down Whitehall. It's not an especially long road, but it takes me ages to get to the end, hobbling and limping, dripping occasional drops of thick, gooey blood from wounds I don't even begin to explore.

I pass Downing Street, once home to the Prime Minister. I know he didn't make it out of London alive — the news programmes mentioned his loss a few times. He hasn't been missed. His cabinet neither. The army runs the country these days.

I wonder if the PM is still inside Number Ten, a zombie like so many of his voters, resting until dark. I could check – the gate is open and unguarded – and probably would any other time. But I'm too weary to care about such trivialities. This country has fallen. Babies are being turned into zombies and feeding on their mothers. Who cares about stuffy politicians now?

Big Ben comes into view. I pause and stare glumly at the clock tower. The hands have stopped at just before a quarter to five. It doesn't chime any more. I doubt it ever will again. A dead clock at the heart of a dead city.

As I edge past the Houses of Parliament, I spot a large red z sprayed near the base of Big Ben, an arrow underneath pointing towards Westminster Bridge. I had planned to turn left and crawl along the riverbank, heading back east to more familiar territory, to see out my time on home turf. But the arrow intrigues me. I've seen others like it during my march west. I think they might be the work of Mr Dowling – he sketched a blood-red z on my cheek when he visited me in my cell in the underground bunker – but I'm not sure. Maybe they were sprayed by humans, survivors hoping to guide others to their hideout. If so, they might be more interested in my offer of assistance than the soldiers were.

Silly old B! Still keen to help the living. Will I never learn?

I move forward, wincing, dragging my left leg, half-blind and itching like crazy. I should have found new clothes and glasses before I came out on to an exposed bridge, but I wasn't thinking clearly. No matter. I push on regardless. I won't be in the sun for long. There will be plenty of shadowy corners for me to rest in on the south side of the river.

I'm surprised, as I advance, to note that the London Eye is still revolving. At first I think it's a trick of the light, so I stop and watch it for a minute. But no, the capsules are moving slowly, just as they did in the old days when every tourist in London made a beeline for its most popular attraction. Today, though, the capsules are deserted. The Eye might be open for business, but it doesn't have any takers.

As I drag myself off Westminster Bridge, I think about the London Dungeon, a place I visited several times when I was alive. I passed its original home earlier in my journey, and now here I am at its subsequent location in County Hall. Maybe that's the place for me. I'd fit in perfectly among all the waxwork monsters.

207

'No,' I whisper. 'You're too grisly. You'd give the rest of the freaks a bad name.'

Shuffling on, I come to the turning for Belvedere Road, which separates the buildings of County Hall, and spot another red z with an arrow beneath, pointing up the road.

I stare wearily at the arrow. I need to feed. It's been a long time since I last ate. I can feel my stomach tightening, my senses beginning to loosen. If I don't tuck into some brains soon, I'll regress and become a mindless revived. If I'm going to follow these damn arrows, I need to make sure I'm in good shape to deal with living humans if I run into any.

St Thomas's Hospital is just behind me, so I turn slowly and make for it. I assumed a hospital would offer rich pickings, but as I work my way through the wards, I find that isn't the case. Others have been here before me and scraped the remains of the corpses dry.

But I've got a bit more up top than your average zombie. As far as I know, any hospital this size has a morgue. And I'm guessing they were normally situated on one of the lower floors, so the staff didn't have to wheel corpses through the rest of the hospital, spooking the life out of everybody.

I find the morgue after a short search but it's locked. It takes me far longer to track down keys for the door, but eventually I find a set in a nurses' cabinet and let myself in. It's brighter and cleaner than I anticipated, no stench of death at all.

The morgue is refrigerated and the electricity is still working. I don't find as many corpses as I thought I might, but four are lying on slabs, ready and waiting, and there are probably a few more tucked away out of sight. If I don't stray from this area in the near future, I can come back and search again. But right now I have more than I need. Time to dine.

I mutter a quick apology over the body of a woman in her early twenties, then chip through her skull with my finger bones and prise out bits of her brain. I eat mechanically, forcing down the food. When I've eaten my fill, I let myself out, lock the door behind me, and throw up in the corridor. I place the keys back where I found them, then return to Belvedere Road, moving more easily than before, but still very far from normal. If my bones and flesh don't heal – and I've no reason to think they will – I'm going to be hobbling like this until the end. No more long jumping or sprinting for me.

I limp along, head low, feeling sorry for myself. As I come to one of the entrances into the main building of County Hall, I notice a small red z sprayed on a wall, the arrow beneath it pointing inwards. I stare at the arrow for a long time, then shrug, mount the steps and push open the unlocked door at the top. If this is a trap, so be it. I'm too tired to worry.

The shade of the building is a welcome relief after being out in the sun. To my surprise there are no zombies here. I thought a massive, dark area like this would be bursting with the undead, but I seem to be the only soul making use of the place.

I wind my way through a warren of corridors and rooms with unbelievably high ceilings. This is like a palace. I never knew there was so much to it. I've been to the aquarium and games arcade at the front of the building in the past, and the London Dungeon, of course, but had no idea that all this existed further back.

Many of the doors are shut and won't open. If I wanted to, I might be able to force them apart or find keys if I searched, but I'm content to simply wander where I can, stepping through every door that opens to me, ignoring the rest.

After a while, I come to a room overlooking the river. I edge up next to the panels of cracked glass and gaze out at one of the best views in town. To my left lie Big Ben, the Houses of Parliament and Westminster Bridge. To my right is a bridge for trains, and just beyond that, Waterloo Bridge. Huge, ornate buildings line the bank on the far side of the river. The London Eye is directly ahead of me, imposing and graceful, still turning smoothly, silently, like some wind-up toy standing tall and proud among the ruins of the city.

I take off my hat and let it drop to the floor. Rubbing the back of my neck, I lean my head against the glass and make a sighing sound. I feel more alone than ever in this immense building, like I'm in a tomb.

Then, as I'm glumly considering where I should turn next, from just behind me, out of the shadows of what was an empty room when I entered, somebody coughs politely and says, 'Good morning, Miss Smith. We've been expecting you.'

To be continued ...